BLISS: FOREVER ELUSIVE & UNIQUE

BLISS:
Forever Elusive & Unique

A collection of short stories

by

WILLIAM M. NATALE

Adelaide Books
New York / Lisbon
2021

BLISS: FOREVER ELUSIVE & UNIQUE
A collection of short stories
By William M. Natale

Copyright © by William M. Natale
Cover design © 2021 Adelaide Books

Published by Adelaide Books, New York / Lisbon
adelaidebooks.org

Editor-in-Chief
Stevan V. Nikolic

For any information, please address Adelaide Books
at info@adelaidebooks.org
or write to:
Adelaide Books
244 Fifth Ave. Suite D27
New York, NY, 10001

ISBN: 978-1-955196-94-9
Printed in the United States of America

Disclaimer
This book is entirely fiction. Any similarity to real individuals
is entirely coincidental.

To Matthew

Also, by William M. Natale

Woolly Wurm, (a children's book)

1968 – A Story as Relevant Today as It Was Then

The Resurrection of Boraichee

Contents

DNA

Oh, jeez, here I was half drunk from wine and a meal laced with a bit of THC making me a bit out of it, sitting on the couch with my trusty dog Sydney, a mere two cushions away also in La-La-Land, slightly snoring embracing hygge on a winter's cold night.

I had binge watched the third season of the marvelous Netflix production of The Crown. Only two days before I had witnessed the Golden Globes and noticed that the series had garnered numerous accolades for a fine piece of storytelling executed with a level of finesse that painstakingly captured the pomp and circumstance of being royal.

Ah, to be a Royal. I assumed before I indulged in the story of the House of Windsor that life would be grand for each of them only to discover that many of them, even the Queen at times suffered great unhappiness.

Happiness? Does such a concept even exist?

And I was disappointed to learn that the Queen often brought great pain to those in her family that were hopelessly in love. In the name of the Crown, she interfered with those who had unfortunately fell in love with someone they *shouldn't have*. And the *"shouldn't have,"* was subjective, not objective but rather prone to court gossip and jesters, media frenzy and the whim of her Majesty.

When it comes to the love of one's life - life doesn't give you many second chances.

The only time I can honestly say I experienced happiness was when I succumbed to being *in love*, which could manifest itself through the touch of a lover, the way a devil inhabits a soul – in a good way. The only *love* I was completely sure of was as a father or paternal figure. Each child bestowed their love on me in their own way and sometimes that bliss was courtesy of my nephews, nieces, grand nephews, grand nieces, and the students I mentored who were kind.

They each took claim to my quest to find happiness and pure unadulterated bliss; each in their own unique shade of DNA.

My First Love

From as far back as I can remember, which would be my 3rd year on Earth, I had always been a bit shy.

You might ask - how did you pick year 3?

Ah! That's easy. You see in my third year of life something very traumatic happened to me. I got hit by a car. One doesn't forget that ever. To this day I still sometimes have dreams that infuse me with a whiter shade of pale as I SEE (not just fantasize) that big old Plymouth eat me up with a bumper that looked like a vein of silver as large as the Whale that ate Jonah. Oh, I still get the sweats from that one.

My first love was to me one of the vestal virgins that I had read about in books that I ingested into my brain in an effort to learn more about the Augustan Age – the World of Rome.

She was so unexpected that perhaps I may have screwed up the opportunity to connect. Shit, I did fuck it up. Even that's complicated because I can't find the words or the reason even if the truth is plain for all to see on how to tell that part of my story. You see, I DID MEET HER just like all my bandmates…oh, didn't I mention the fact that I was in a band? Well, everyone was in those days. It was a surefire way to meet chicks as we used to say back in the day.

The scene - ah, yes, I'm afraid I still think via a mind saturated with the world of television and film production - the way I'm used to telling a tale. So please forgive me if I indulge myself. As I was saying – the scene was set in the basement of where I lived. I lived with my parents as do all of us in our teen years even including the ones after graduating from high school. We were set to practice – a band with three guitars and a drummer. I was the drummer.

Unbeknownst to me, the bass player, Michael or Mick as we called him had suggested to his girlfriend that she bring a girl or two to our practice. We rarely had visitors listen to us as we practiced, so this was a big deal made even bigger (hmmmm – I didn't mean that – ha-ha – yes I did) – SO MUCH BIGGER because the opposite sex would be coming…coming to listen to us…and there wasn't a man amongst us that didn't tingle a bit knowing that…expecting that…anticipating that…that spark that ignites when men and women copulate – whether only in their minds or not. One way or another, we knew that one of us would probably not have a partner to tag along with after the practice, but, hope springs eternal in the hearts of young red-blooded American males.

I had my eyes on her and she had her eyes set on mine. When we took a break, she came up to talk to me. I liked that. She could have turned to the other two solos like me but she didn't. So how much of an idiot was I when I turned seasick upon hearing Mick's girl, Sue, proclaim, "Let's get some pizza," which I ignored feigning an illness I didn't have unless you count shyness. DUH! And I hadn't had a hit the entire night.

And so, the *girl* with the flaming red hair gave her number to one of my bandmates. Of course, that was to be expected but knowing that made me seasick all over again. How was it that I couldn't stand because I didn't have the sea legs necessary to keep me stable when the *woman* in that *girl* turned my mind upside down?

That's why I was surprised to receive a phone call from the flaming red hair *girl*. She was inviting me to meet her for coffee. I asked, "When?" I probably should have asked, "How'd you get my number?" I should have said, "No thank you – aren't you already taken?" But I found I couldn't refuse. You see, I thought she might want to talk about my bandmate, perhaps quiz me on what he liked or didn't like, on his favorite things as if somehow the *red hair girl* needed my help to understand my amigo. I didn't want to play a character from a movie where everyone sang about their favorite things…I think that was from "The Sound of Music," but then maybe not…my memory isn't what it used to be….ah, that's bullshit, my mind was and still IS as sharp as a clock on THC - that damn ditty was in that 1965 film classic.

So, hell there was no reason for me not to accept the invitation to meet. If I felt uncomfortable, I would invoke the creed adhered to by all males which required me to regretfully ask. "Say, red hair *girl,* I thought you were going out with…

"I am."

Wow, that was shocking. Holy Shit, I was way over my head. I knew it and so did she and I know that she knew that she knew it, which really made me shit-sick on top of my sea sickness.

We were walking through the outer student union mecca when I felt her hand in mine and I went "HA-WA-I -eeeeeeee!" I actually felt a bit of that Beatle joy and it wasn't hard for me to give her a look that only two souls blissfully connected transmit via eyes that are locked in the look of love. And if you don't get that shade of pale then let me put it to you this way – the two love birds were ebullient in HAPPINESS. That kind of look – and if that don't make you a bit erect or wet then frankly, you're DEAD.

And, so began a romance that was intense. We both didn't want to cross a line that had no ability to reverse…so we never ventured farther than a point we couldn't take back. The *girl* with the flaming red hair was on my mind constantly. To the credit of the *girl* with the red flaming hair, she convinced me that we had to come clean with the bandmate who got her phone number first. And so that's what we did, which made our world even weirder.

In the end there were a number of cigarettes burned while WE sat in my Chevy talking about - or in my case listening – to an inquisition that included these beauties: Where were WE headed? Had WE set a course? Were WE leaving for the coast? What were WE doing? It was the dreaded, "What are WE doing?" CONVERSATION.

I could have lied but God knows I would have died. If there was one thing I wasn't going to give up, it was my self-respect. I was such a fool, the kind that would give up the *girl*, rather than be dishonest. The truth was simply, without question, plain to SEE. WE or should I say ME and the *girl*, weren't in sync when the inquisition was over. I sure as shit knew it, so did she, and I knew that she knew that I knew that she knew… and that was sad…truly sad.

I got a card not long after that smoky, steaming, (yes, there had been some steaming prior to the CONVERSATION) evening. The envelope was huge. It was an oversized envelope with a whole bunch of postage on it. But it was a thin envelope and I was sure it might be some kind of advert or yes, hopefully a card. And, so it was - a beautiful card. The card was oversized to accommodate a dreamy looking image that had been infused into that cardboard like paper. A bird…on a branch with a red coat like that flaming hair, that CARDINAL RED hair. There may have been a leaf or two - but they were yellow…like piss yellow and most of the branches were empty. I couldn't help but feel a bit seasick since I could read what others couldn't see. I knew that *girl,* and this time she knew that I knew what she was trying to say without saying it and that I knew that she knew that I knew. I wandered through the interior of the card and read what my vestal virgin (and she was still a virgin after our fandango) had to share. WOW! I hadn't expected such a dispatch.

Sorry, you'll never know, and I will always know that you'll never know and unfortunately you must know that I know that you know that?

Some tales should go to the grave. NO? (of course, I mean OUI?).

Why Did He Have to Die so Young?

The Beatle's song, "In My Life," is so eerie and yet, you must admit that the lyrics are spot on in conveying how you feel about those you loved who have passed before you into the pale blue shade of everlasting LIFE – whatever that is…and trust me, I've already passed into the beyond and there's something so sublime and peaceful that I really didn't want to have to return to Mother Earth as ghostly or in the flesh…Oh MY GOD – I just wanted so bad to pass on.

And I know many who wonder if there is anything else that challenged me for believing as I do so concretely. But if truth be told, I didn't hold any fear as a young tyke of 3; I got to see life here and there by accident as I found myself in the same spot in space and time which lead to an explosion upon impact with that big old car about to engulf me and yet FEAR wasn't a factor. If anything, I felt nothing but sheer exhilaration, sheer peace and a whiter shade of heaven that I absolutely/concretely felt ONE with. OMG…I had seen the ghostly face of truth and I was blessed to know at so young what many never ever discover – ever/never/evermore as the Raven might crow…or am I getting my metaphors mixed up? Either way, I knew what they didn't, and they probably thought I experienced it the same way they did when in fact I didn't. I was free of doubt. "God have mercy on their poor souls," I devilishly whispered.

But, when you have a bandmate caught up in the quandary as to whether he gets to stay on Mother Earth or he must leave – facing testicular cancer that is dissipating him, you wonder if you have any business of sharing your insight with a man that probably doesn't want to hear that you've seen the other side and it's beautiful when he already enjoys the beauty of a loving wife and a baby boy while only being 19, a tender age at that.

And while my stricken bandmate was doing all of that, he was also going to the Illinois Institute of Technology, a.k.a. IIT, a prestigious university studying something very scientific, so scientific that I can no longer remember – but I will never forget the great promise my bandmate should have experienced in his future. So why does my friend who is younger than me in that moment in time by a full year find himself on a dead-end road that needed to be enveloped by miracle, oracle, miraculous shades of pale for the journey to continue on Mother Earth? That question was answered by departure. For those left behind, one then becomes one of those characters in the musical notes of The Beatles, "In My Life."

But life moved on and I found myself on a double date with of all people, *MyFirstLove* and her husband – the bandmate I lost her to – along with the wife of our beloved DEPARTED bandmate. As I was directed to take her home (hint-hint), I wound up being alone with the young widow. And we all know what's coming next…yes, we did the nasty and frankly I know I disappointed the wife of my beloved DEPARTED on the physical side of that equation, but on the mental side, we were simpatico. We talked and talked and talked and drank red wine as we cozied up to one another; I think that meant more to the wife of my beloved DEPARTED than my lack of finesse in the car bedroom. Thankfully that did come later for me but on that hot August night, I think I cooled the firestorm that maybe burned a bit in her wanton need for raw, raw hard out of control mad sex. But perhaps, I'm putting too much weight on that part of the relationship? Oh, my God, I should have been on Oprah as one of those gentlemen who really knew how to be GAY with a woman. Women love GAY GUYS, and everyone must have their GAY GUY which could be heterosexual providing they understood the importance of listening like a GAY GUY. TRY it sometime gents and you'll see what I mean. BUT I must insist that she was not mad at me; she was mad at her beloved DEPARTED for leaving so early. They had been together a mere 3 years…you know that's got to hurt.

And I am sad to say that I never followed up with the wife of my beloved DEPARTED…and damn it - I now regret that. We didn't necessarily have to become a couple but having lost someone we both loved, we could have loved each other a little better. And I'll take 90% of that but the wife of my beloved DEPARTED owns 10% for that loss. There was no reason for us to never connect again and for that I felt so awful that when I could some 15 years later reunite via a high school reunion – I didn't. All of THIS was a good deal before social media, so a reunion was the preferred way to rediscover Betty Lou or Suzie Q.

Yeah, in painful admission I admit that's mainly on me, and my greatest concern is that she or I will pass on, and we won't even be as good as two ships passing through the night.

Here's what I do know. The wife of my beloved DEPARTED got married again and together they raised the son of my beloved DEPARTED. They lived somewhere in a nearby suburb…and the only way I knew any of that is that MyFirstLove told me that when she and her husband returned to town to see mother-in-law and mother respectively.

So…what did I learn? That sometimes you're only meant to be a MOMENT – but that MOMENT when it breathed life, was a breath well worth taking.

It's complicated… like the South Atlantic Anomaly is complicated…yeah, that fuckin' complicated because – BECAUSE - when it comes to love, what can one say but, "Heyyyyyyy, it's uh…you know…complicated."

A Girl Who Loves *Mountain* Can't Be All Bad

Everyone knew her as Cooch. Cooch was a teenager that lived about 2 blocks away from my house. Someone in the band, oh yeah, the guy who married MyFirstLove, had a girlfriend up that way that all the guys fell in love with. Karen was a chestnut brunette with blond highlights who didn't need the dye to make her hair shine and shine it did. Rumpelstiltskin would have wanted strands of Karen's long lustrous hair; it was that gorgeous. Cooch had dropped by one night with a few other girls, Cathy & Christina.

Cathy was like one of those actresses that get tagged with that innocuous if not annoying term, "America's Sweetheart." You know who gets those monikers? Girls that are perky…perky smile, perky tits, perky eyes, just fucking PERKY. So, yes, she was eye candy but the kind of candy that is crafted by hand, because if there ever was a Doris Day (a '50's/'60's movie Goddess that was also a Miss Goody-Two-Shoes), it was Cathy. Beautiful but elusive and yet so accessible in the minds of male fans - and if we're honest - females that chose to suppress that notion of lust to a closet. That's just how it was back then.

Christina was quieter. She had an inner beauty that one could envelop themselves in through her eyes. I beg of you don't misconstrue my description. Christina was a classic beauty, the kind one might find in LITTLE WOMEN or PRIDE & PREJUDICE.

Christina also had a kid. A kid she would not give up. She and her kid were a package and I found that out on our very first date. I wasn't in the marrying mood at that moment. Shit I still wanted to sow some wild oats. But there was something so sweet about the lass that I just could not resist. I fell in love with her…oh, now that felt good…and I'm not even talking about the sex. There was something in the glint of her eyes when they peered or rather bored through mine to my inner soul at peace wrapped in the sweet love of someone who knew me well enough to understand that I lusted for that soft feminine pink shade of pale. Yeah, lust is the word because it sure beats rust which often happens in a relationship and we're not having that here in this fairy tale. Because love stories should be so much more!

Love stories are fairy tales. You have to find someone or maybe they have to find you. Those kinds of odds are tough enough but then somehow two ships passing through life now sail what? Parallel? One behind the other? How BAD does DADDY really want it? And you're still questioning my proclamation of what constituted a fairy tale?

So much has to go RIGHT….and that happened for Christina and me…at least that's what I thought.

We had a blast or so I thought on the night we went to see *MOUNTAIN* – the rock group…you know the band that does a kickass *Mississippi Queen*. Ah, so you do recall the tune. Yes, a great feast of fine music, a hit or two of mind-bending THC and the cuddling of two souls in that soft pink shade of pale. What more does anyone want? I couldn't help but become seasick when she said, "I'm going to miss you. I'm going back with my baby's father. We're going to try and re-locate the shade of pale that once made us one…one family." She wept as she softly said. "I'm sorry."

Wow, my soft pink shade of pale turned darker and darker. I'm not sure I ever got over her. God, I loved kissing Christina! Oh, those soft, soft, lips – so soft and filled with that soft pink shade of pale. I wasn't seasick when I had all of that…it was only after I lost all of that…but Christina made the right move. God love her! And I couldn't help it. She always had a piece of my heart, that I don't think any of those I fell in love after her could restore.

She was after all - my soft pink shade of pale.

A Fairy Tale Love Story Not Told Linearly

No, we just won't have any of that LINEARLY progression. Instead, let's take this ride down that RABBIT HOLE that allows one to traverse through time and dimension.

There is no love of a child as great as that of the grand MA-MA. At least that's what your mother or mother-in-law has reminded you of many times - no?

Nevertheless, in this case, it was true! As true as you can have these days in a conflicted world.

Grandma Rose had my big brother and me, in her lap at the age of 72. There was no way she could have taken the girl… who I later found out was our sister. SIS lived with our other Grand MA Ma on the west side of town.

So, I can only attest to my impressions of my Grand MA Ma, who I felt was the sweetest Grand MA Ma anyone would be blessed to have. And I thank God daily for my Grand MA MA and our daily bread and ask that we be forgiven for complaining about our lives that are devoid of the frustrations and heart aches my ROSA had to deal with at such a senior age. Need I repeat the fact that ROSA was 72, dealing with two tykes, who may have been nice but c'mon, we're talking about boys. But in spite of all that I think Grand MA MA loved it. We adored her and she adored us. Oh, My GOD - can you ask for anything more? ROSA was the matriarch but in a good way… she certainly had a wonderful shade of pale. And Oh-My-GOD, (sorry but everyone's got a CRUTCH) – SO – Oh-My-God, her hand made ravioli was divine! I know everyone says that about their beloved and when you think about that, I don't mind – do YOU? You don't! Aww…that's sweet!

One of my favorite memories at a wee-wee age was helping Grand MA-MA load up the ravioli. I did that by grabbing with my wee-wee fingers little bits of spinach, or it could have been little bits of cheese, or it could have been little bits of porcini – you know – mushrooms - or whatever ROSA set her heart to create. I intentionally left out in that last sentence the word Grand MA MA before the nomenclature of our beloved, ROSA. Now why did I do that? Could it be that ROSA look gorgeous and eternally young when she showered us with love served on a cloud of sunlight crystals, blinding rays and dazzling diamonds? It's complicated…but what the heck, we've got the time? Si?

My mother was an RN – a registered nurse. Let's all admit it. We're already in love with someone who is self-sacrificing and caring. In the era known as the world of drumpf, that concept sometimes feels so distant…so very remote. I hate to admit it but as a kid I wanted that shade of pale better known simply as unconditional love. I was looking for love at that tender age, wondering what happened to MOMMY? Even if we – my brother and I – were remarkably young, we both felt that loss of MOMMY. That's why I always loved bathing in that soft pink shade of pale that was so ROSA…such a sweet soul that when I think about it now as an old man, I can truly appreciate what that fine woman went through to help her son and her daughter-in-law and their three children, her grandkids.

If anybody knew the importance of family, ROSA did. She became a widow not long after she wed a man that she loved and pleased to bear him a son, my uncle, my father's brother and... well, you get the idea.

Uh, huh, so you think. But I see your uh-uh skeptical that *this perception could be realized by a mere tyke* and I appreciate the fact that children and DOGS (yes DOGS) – I say SO – yay SYDNEY! MY SWEET, SWEET SYDNEY, the sweetest Gonczy you'll ever meet - sorry, but hey – who doesn't love SYDNEY? Right? Ah, now, what did I see?

I saw how my ROSA looked at my Uncle Bobby. Maybe it was her first born, I don't know? But even as a kid I could see a look filled with passion. I never saw Grand MA MA look at my dad that way...and yet she loved him – all of him including us - and it was evident. We lived in Grand MA MA's two-flat building. Grand MA MA was absolutely grand when it came to how she sacrificed for my father and his wife and their three kids. She took the back end of the 2nd floor with no more than a kitchen and a bedroom. She shared the bathroom that was perfectly located, between the first 75% of the second floor of the flat and the other 25%. How convenient! There was a small hallway – with doors to either side of the flat – and then a door to the bathroom. And Grand MA MA owned the building - BUT - being magnanimous - she took less to give more to those she loved.

The plan was a compromise of sorts. My father was wary that someone from DCFS (Dept. of Children & Family Services) would come knocking on the door asking, "How are the children doing?" That question could have been answered with one word, "Fine," but it never was. DCFS was not an agency you could tinker with and before you knew it, they would break up a family till the other parent returned from the TB Sanitarium or was declared dead – which – was a very common occurrence prior to the advent of a cure. Losing a beloved to consumption (what they then called TB) was not new to ROSA, her new husband Giovanni, her son Bobby conceived with in love with her first husband and her other son, our dad. As a family they lost a little girl, Maria at the tender age of four to TB. Today, even in the 21st Century, the number one killer in the world is Tuberculosis.

Bobby had been given the keys to the store front building with a flat above it and a garage with a pit from which one could work on the underpinnings of an automobile. The store front was a tire store that both brothers eventually worked out of to make a living before the world came crashing down as did the stock market and the fortunes of many Americans. Fortunately, the property was paid for, so even though the business went south, the building didn't. How did immigrants with little to their name amass as much as they did? Sacrifice.

I'm not sure what Uncle Bobby did after the tire shop floated away but I do know that for my dad, he found his passion working for the Chicago Fire Department.

MOMMY's exile was hard on everyone. But in some ways, I believe it was especially hard on my father. I know from the way he looked at my mother, a technique I picked up as a tyke, giving one's spirit the ability to see the nuances of the shades of pale; we all possessed "it" – just some of us knew we had "it" and others never saw that potential. I knew that FATHER FIRE-FIGHTER burned mad alchemy in his heart for MOMMY. Who wouldn't? She was *girl next door* pretty with a pleasing smile. She had a soft voice. She was always concerned about everyone in her family and even extended that to those she didn't know well – like her patients. In my heart I was convinced even then that MOMMY's every waking moment painted on a snowflake to be unveiled when the cold winds blew would comprise a portrait of a sweet, sweet face that blossomed with the softest, pink shade of pale. Her eyes were so inviting that I can see them now in my mind, directing me to showcase whatever talent I might have to tell the story of why LOVE is so consuming and yet so exhilarating.

And so, I have the softest of soft spots in my heart for both my *Grand MA MA's- MA Ma's*. My other GRAND MA Ma, Hazel, was not in good health. She took in my sister, who was six-and-five-years senior to her brothers. Hazel had Grand PA PA to help and I'm sure he did. I just don't know a lot about what my sister went through, since we were miles apart literally and figuratively.

In those days, you did what you had to do. So, the old man had his alderman, a real press hound known by all, serve as his attorney when they met with DCFS. DCFS was startled that anyone would dare take them to court but also terrified that they now could face in court an attorney who just happened to also be a very powerful alderman who might make them pay even if they won the case. So, the gauntlet had been thrown and now it was merely a case of working out a compromise when it came to the firefighter's kids with the TB wife. If DCFS tried to muscle our father, his attorney would have muscled back – not once but 7 times as much – wait – is that the drumpf algebraic equation? I can't remember if it's 7 or 6 times. Oh well, either way, it would have been a tantrum.

And so, the compromise was that sister would be exiled to the other Grand MA Ma. DCFS absolutely put their foot down on that one. "C'mon Captain, your mother Rosa is 72 – give her a break – she is your mother – right?"

Ooooh, knowing my father as I do, that last tidbit with the condescending scale of tones applied in the form of, "She is your mother," would be construed as fighting words. And you never wanted to get into a fight with my father. The only one who ever won a fight with my father was my mother. Even Grand MA MA didn't hold that distinction. It was the woman with the smoky hazel eyes who always got my father to do whatever she wanted; maybe not at first, but all in good time my pretty. The old man was a sucker for that soft pink shade of pale my mother exuded when she smoldered a look that cut him to the quick with either joy or anguish, dependent on my father's behavior.

My MOMMY had her share of scars and scares. That's what you can expect when you marry a firefighter, because PA-PA at times walked on that fine line between here and there or a.k.a. the hereafter. That's why she always LOOKED at him - REALLY LOOKED at him as if it might be the final time she LOOKED at the love of her life - alive and well — the man that filled her shade of pale with LOVE, sweet-sweet LOVE…the fairy tale ending noting that *they lived happily ever after* which at one time the world adored before it's residents became so cynical. They were the sultans of honky-tonk romance and you couldn't help but love it. Oh yeah, they had their fights and they were good at that too…very livid and oh so passionate!

Despite my ingenue mind, in my eyes they were the shining example of a successful marriage. I can remember as a teenager having a dream of me in my late 20's. I was smiling in my three-piece suit with a beautiful wife next to me in a sheer looking pastel Paris fashion with two small kids, a boy and a girl in that 3 ½ -4-5 age range. There were large evergreen bushes neatly trimmed behind us. It was the kind of shot you frame, that's how nice it was!

I wanted what my father had. A beautiful, loving wife. What I failed to realize was how antiquated that idea was. What my father expected from a wife was in keeping with how many women felt - not all - but enough who had the gene known as *service* or those who may have been indoctrinated by the women in their life to run their households and men that GO IKE way.

Something in my MOMMY must have come undone with her health but with the help of my father's alderman/ attorney, MOMMY got a bed at the Sanitarium. We were never allowed to go to the Sanitarium although we saw pictures that our dad had taken with a Kodak. I remember how white that Sanitarium looked. It was almost as if we were looking at our MOMMY the Angel; it was that white! And MOMMY would write us letters which brought sheer howls of joy. C'mon you're a tyke, you don't get mail and you know that. Only the adults get mail. So, mail was a big thing in a little life.

MOMMY's letters were more or less always the same. She'd start out with her profession of love and she was so good at changing it up with every letter. Then she'd bring up something that dad must have revealed. If it was a rift between me and my brother, MOMMY didn't command, she didn't have to...her gentle words said it all. "Be kind. Be nice. Don't waste MOMMY's time...time is so precious." I didn't realize the gravity of the situation, neither did my brother. Maybe our sister did, being a-bit-older. But I sensed something in my father's eyes, in my mother's eyes when she would visit – never entering the house wearing a mask and looking at us gathered on the front porch, a good ten feet from where she stood. What I will never forget is how they looked like two souls desperately trying to hold on to each other. I may have been a tyke but even I couldn't help but notice.

My father was told by the doctors that he had best get his wife's affairs in order and that he best figure out how to deal with the children. A lot of "bests" were doled out in addition to those primary concerns.

And that's when the miracle happened. A tale that you can either dismiss or consider because when you hear it, you'll no doubt wonder how all those coincidences occurred and lined up just right for a chance at redemption to live a full life with a husband and three kids – a family she loved with all her breath and all her heart. That does sound like a fairy tale and we all know that you'll only find fairy tales in books, but there are a few cases where the personal anecdote can actually be more satisfying than that which you'll find in Grimm's Fairy Tales… my apologies to Jacob and Wilhelm Grimm.

MOMMY was enlisted to be part of a test, a scientific experiment to check the effectiveness of a new drug that supposedly could cure Tuberculosis or at least keep it in check so that it didn't ravage and destroy one's body. What MOMMY didn't know was that she was to be in the control group – the damned who would get placebos instead of the potential cure. But MOMMY had been a nurse, a caregiver who had put her life on the line dealing with infectious patients saddled with all sorts of maladies including terrifying TB that destroyed one's ability to breathe. That kindness didn't go unnoticed by the RN doling out the medication who had also at one time worked at that same Mercy Hospital where MOMMY contracted her dreadful disease when a patient, she was tending to upchucked sputum filled with germs that then attacked our beloved Angel.

Maybe it was my father's daily prayers to the Almighty for a remedy or perhaps his unrelenting spirit to never give up that he instilled in all of us or maybe it was the MERCY of that RN, who decided that MOMMY needed a break. Whatever it was, the RN who held the keys to the kingdom decided she was going to break protocol for her comrade in arms and MOMMY got the good stuff and miraculously recovered.

Whenever I reminisce about MOMMY's ordeal, it's pure bliss to realize that despite all odds sometimes miracles do happen with a little bit of help from a Spirit that rejoices the beat of a kind heart.

The Girl Next Door or Maybe a Couple of Blocks Away

I'm not sure I have *ever* told anyone about this love…or maybe it was more of a quest for love that I knew deep down, I didn't stand a chance at getting.

I saw her coming out of mass. She was blonde but not that dumb kind of blonde misnomer that afflicted even smart blondes. Somehow, I just knew she was smart, and I was right. But she was shy and frankly even more shy than me. What caught my breath was her face. She was just so luminous, her skin so shimmering with pink, pink, pink – a soft pink glow that could be experienced even in the full light of day.

She did not smile much, although she had a beautiful set of teeth with ivory that was so bright it often *refrackted* – I like the non-existent word better than the way I initially wrote it, *so bright it often reflected sunlight into sparkles.*

We went out on about four dates. We mainly went to the movies and maybe grabbed a bite to eat or ice cream. She did kiss me when I walked her to the door (that's old school but girls like that shit). And then upon the conclusion of our fourth date she shared the news. "I'm leaving for Northern on Sunday." Northern Illinois University was in faraway De Kalb. Frankly it's really not that far – some 50 miles outside of Chicago but that's 100 miles of driving to see a - *girl* - and as much as I would have wanted to, I couldn't afford it. For fuck's sake, I was a college student, just like her trying to make it through the week on what I made on a part time job.

So mainly I continued our relationship via correspondence, which I mistakenly considered romantic. The Internet and cellular which affords us texting, emailing, and communication via numerous apps wasn't part of the scene back in that day. I did call, which was expensive at the time and disappointing since she always seemed so busy and "couldn't talk." By now you're all saying, "What the fuck is wrong with this guy? Doesn't he get it? HEY – DON'T YOU GET IT? C'mon man don't make it this HARD — she's just not that INTO YOU bro."

But to the credit or detriment of those in my circle I never heard those dismissive words.

When she came home, I made the most of the time of her break doing things she wanted to do. That was the truth – which was plain to see by everyone but me. I was naively still mesmerized by that soft pink glow of her face. I could have melted into such an enticing face…a face that makes you feel loved because it's that hypnotic…well, at least that's how her *look* affected me. I was in love with that *look*. But let's be frank, the kind of look we're talking about has to be cinema approved…sort of the look between Bogie & Lauren that melted the celluloid of the film forcing the directors of their movies to do additional takes. Wow! Those two – that sizzling couple had at least in MYTH if not downright in TRUTH one hell of a LOVE… one of those loves that if you're lucky the Grand Wizard of munchkin land mercifully bestows on you. This is the LOVE you take and hold until your dying breath because this love …THIS LOVE – changed my shade of pale to an effervescent glow that just engulfed me with the golden, most golden moment of my short and novel romantic life…a love affair you think you'll never forget.

At the conclusion of a date on my birthday of all days, the second day of January, just before her departure back to Northern that same night, Miss Pink Shade of Pale handed me an envelope and made me promise that I would obey the notations clearly marked in lipstick on the envelope.

Don't Open – Till - I Leave for NIU. I'll call you and tell you when I'm hitting the road back.

She said all that with a smile showing off those pearly white ivories.

That's the only thing I ever wondered about. What was with the smile? I couldn't help but fret that she might dump me…I was always so worried about losing her. I wondered why she couldn't just say that to my face. Those cryptic instructions bothered me. But hope struck this young man's fancy with the notion that if she was considering a time-out, somehow, I'd be able to convince her that we really were good together.

Really? Wow, in hindsight it's so clear to see that I was lost - but maybe it's also fair to say with age comes wisdom, a wisdom you can't fathom when caught up in dreams that deal with a pretty woman with a pink glow. If that was her intention the only good thing was I wouldn't have to wait for weeks till the next break to find out. Fate would visit me that very night. I missed her call but caught instructions delivered via that sweet voice of hers that I could indeed open the envelope. My heart was hopeful since she sounded so pleasant. But the note made it clear when it was addressed to Dear John – I'm not a John but you know what I mean. We were no longer dark chocolate & almonds, connected by an ampersand. Do you know how ridiculous that sounds? Anyway, who was I kidding. I knew this day was coming and I'd no longer be a "happening" kind of guy with the beautiful blond on my arm. Holy Shit! I was devastated having lost my selfish wants and desires.

I left the kitchen where the phone and the answering machine resided in my parents' home and walked out to the living room where my dad had the late TV newscast on. I decided to say good night to the old man and head for bed when I heard the anchor say, "There's been a deadly accident on I-90 West at the De Kalb exit to NIU. A young man and woman were in a car that slid off a ramp encased with ice due to the inclement weather. It was reported that they were boy-friend and girlfriend, both attending NIU." I didn't recognize the name of the male driving the car, but I knew the name of the female-passenger.

I know this sounds bizarre, but I couldn't help but wonder if I'd be invited to the wake. Did her folks know she was dumping me? They both seemed to like me but maybe I got that wrong as well.

I don't know how else to say it - and yeah, I know it makes me sound like a Dick …but the fact is I HURT to discover she was with another guy. However, I did know, oh but I knew that *she* didn't deserve that even if the way *she* treated me was anything but a pink shade of pale.

I cried a river that night and I hate to say it, but I worried more about me than what and where *she* was and in what shade of pale, she now found herself in. I prayed that the guy she departed with was worthy of her love. That's the way it would be in a fairy tale if it was up to me. So, why couldn't it be that way in real life? That's what I wanted for my-heart-throb-of-a-love, so that she found herself in a brilliant white shade of pale glowing with gold...the gold that comes with sheer, utter, un-abashing, unassuming contentment, peace and love that must be true.

God love her! I knew I had and yet I couldn't help but laugh at my ineptitude when it came to reading a woman. But it was a thrill to be in love even if the love wasn't reciprocal... with time comes the ability to tell a "tale" honestly.

And isn't that why we're engaged now...for me to tell you a story and hopefully one filled with bliss? Now that would be SOMETHING and a tale worth telling! So please forgive me for telling something a bit macabre but one that left a mark on me about a young woman that looked so wonderful to me every time we were together...even that last night. Who knows? Maybe we'll meet again and if we do, I'll thank her for being a gentle soul even if her honesty hurt and for being the first woman, I fell in love with...that can't all be bad.

The Babe in the Blue Medical Frock

I knew it as soon as I saw her that I would DO IT with her. I think she knew it too. But until we got to that knot, we were both tiptoeing around each other in a lab in a hospital on a main thoroughfare on the northwest side of the metropolis. Kismet had somehow brought us together.

She was cute! She had a wrinkle in her smile, a crinkle in her effervescent eyes, and her porcelain doll skin glowed with a shade of pale that captured my soul. She had eyelashes that could literally wink in Morse code the words, "FUCK ME…I'M FUCK-A-BLE," over and over with a staccato rhythm that produced a percussive caused by the brush of those eyelashes… hmm, I could eat those fuckin' eyelashes. But having said all of that, I was hooked on someone who never ever realized how sexy she really was…and that had to be frustrating.

I got that job in the medical lab through the help of a sibling initially.

At that time a hospital didn't have to hire certified technicians. A college student taking science classes with the possibility of going into MED school or seeking their certification could work in the lab. As you can imagine, that didn't sit well with those who were certified because our pre-med positions allowed the hospital to get our work for a good deal less.

It's always economics, isn't it?

But for whatever reason I never got that from the girl with the fuckable eyes. If anything, she taught me little tricks with tips that truthfully brought the best out in me. I knew I had no intent of making lab work my life's work…but for now, it had its perks and she definitely was one of them.

Both of us were living at home, both of us college students. Ms. Fuckable eyes had also studied in her junior and senior years in high school how to become a certified lab technician. She was light years ahead of me and even some of those with their certifications. As a guy, I was light years behind her, but a guy who instinctively knew how to survive during a recession and one who could be inventive if need be to get employment. And so it was inevitable that I had to ask myself, "Self, does any one of your buddies have a crib where my new-found-baby and I can rock? Fortunately, I had a guy. You need a guy for sports tickets, sometimes parking tickets and sometimes for other things important to red blooded American males?

Anyway, my guy's name was *Phil the Scanman*. Note the spelling of the last word of the previous sentence carefully because *scam* isn't a part of it. Phil's expertise was in his ability to *scan* – he was big time into x-ray and something still a bit new at the time - ultrasound. The doctors respected Phil. He had several ultrasound rigs, some that were huge when he first started out and as time went by, they often were no more than the size of a laptop. Phil worked a lot and so his small apartment was, shall we say, *available*?

Actually, the apartment was basement bound and very small…but Phil had a nice big bed and me and Ms. Fuckable Eyes – literally spent every hour we could together fucking each other's brains out. We both loved sex. There never was any talk about what we were going to do the tomorrow after the next tomorrow. We really lived in the present.

I don't often get to live in the present. I'm too damn worried about the future.

And as someone living in the present with Ms. Fuckable while still a young vibrant man, I was unfortunately getting seasick, no joke, seriously and not in connection with the finer sex but something known as the "disembarkment syndrome." It's a disorder of rocking vertigo and imbalance when you skip the light fandango.

Ah, those were the days and I did feel *present* everywhere and anywhere I was with her. We both knew deep down we were not going to become inseparable mates. The only sadness I have is how we ended it. At the end, we both cheated, but I caught her cheating and that's when I said, "I have to break this off."

I heard a tiny of tiniest sighs and then in a whisper the word, "Why?"

I even found out the guy's name…it was Woody. I had no idea who Woody was…I just knew he was giving my Fuckable Eyes a ride on his Woody. And so, I confronted her.

"So, who's Woody?"

Her porcelain skin turned red as a rush of corpuscles slammed into those pretty as pink cheeks. She peered at me with those eyes, except this time their color turned to *scorn*…and *scorn* is not a kumbaya kind of color you want to be anywhere near.

"There is no reason for us to do this. So, you got me. But I also got you because I know."

She looked me in the eyes without the *scorn* and nodded. I knew she knew. She just didn't know the name of my fellow sinner-in-FUCK.

We ran into each other literally in a shopping mall some eight years later. We did hug and she had quite the rock on her finger and was dressed impeccably. Her smile was dazzling…she always had this impish look about her that was so, so, so – sexy.

I was in my usual casual jean look from eight years earlier. But I think we both liked where we were – where we wound up. We were two very different people, but we were simpatico even if no longer lovers.

It was plain to see that we had been better for each other by not being with each other…at least that's what I tried to convince myself to accept even though I didn't truly believe it. But life moves on.

Ah, but those eyes!

What's Love Got to Do with It?

I found myself engaged at way too young of an age. What was I doing? But I was head-over-heels as they note in every fairy tale, so why not mine? I had been smitten and I blame it on the flaming red hair. As a boy, I had dreams of being with a beautiful woman with red hair that was as flaming as the sun refracted or reflected (if we're using correct English) through it - almost a crimson shade of pale. In my dream, RED and I, were surrounded by two very cute little girls, one 4 or 5 years older than the youngest.

Both girls were wearing dresses made of midnight blue velvet and white lace that exuded a bluish tint of pale. RED donned something sheer, something that made her look transparently thin. RED often said, there are only two things women really want. To be thin with breathtaking beauty and to never have to want for anything…the first part of that sentence before the conjunction was all woman…the last part was all man and what could he bring to the table. At least that's how it was in my fairy tale dream.

In my vision, RED was every bit an envision and mystery as Orhan Pamuk's, "The Woman with The Red Hair." I just couldn't appreciate that in my younger years never having had the experience of reading that masterpiece to discuss it over wine and pasta with my good friends in the *Wine About Books* - book club. Being in a book club was not something I did when I was young. I realized I had missed the fun that comes with that membership for the major portion of my life. I'm sure there are book clubs with younger people; I never took advantage of it nor did I even try to find out if such clubs exist. I assume they do.

So that's how my family was dressed in my dream. I wore a very executively built three-piece suit that signified I'd become a BIG SHOT. I've yet to meet a man, not to be confused with a saint, who doesn't quest for one day becoming a BIG SHOT, whether that's measured in money, prestige, power or whatever cardinal sin you fancy.

For some reason I can't seem to remember the color of my cloth, nor can I remember my aura…my shade of pale. RED's shade of pale was fabulous in its crimson hues and purple hazes. The girls perspired here comes the sun kind of vibes that made their shade of pale a soft blue sky kind of glow that I felt as warm. Like Daniel Hillard in Mrs. Doubtfire, which Robin Williams portrayed before he fabricated the character - Mrs. Doubtfire – adapted from the book Madame Doubtfire for the screen, I too loved my kids passionately in my dreams and in my life. I always knew I wanted to have kids…always!

Well, in *that* real world…not *that* fairy tale, it became painfully clear in the dating game that I couldn't compete with RED's best friend's boyfriend…or should I say middle age plus male partner and then later husband/guy…that sounds a bit CATTY doesn't it? Well, that's because it's supposed to be CATTY.

George was a tall Greek Gentleman who also owned a restaurant and several apartment buildings. He always seemed to have a tan and in-his-eyes…but just in his eyes…you couldn't help but see or catch the wave that was Cary Grant…dashing Cary Grant the movie icon. That was George.

So how does a young guy about to graduate from college compete with a guy like that?

So, you say? Why can't you be a brother-at-arms? You both are with women who love each other.

It wasn't that easy. I just hated hearing how much of a BIG SHOT – George was. I wanted to hear how much of a BIG SHOT, I was. Remember…that's always in the dream, that family-of-four shot capturing a moment in time when everyone in the frame of that Kodachrome looks utterly smashing – a visual – I held not only in my mind but in my heart. That's why it hurt and RED never got that, never.

But whenever the grass looks greener on the 18th hole, you often find out on the 19th – at the bar that all isn't really as green as it appears. George and I actually became confidantes who now and then would catch a drink together. We knew the score. George had money. I still had my youth, and no matter how much money anyone has, they can't buy their youth back; but they can sure die trying.

George was a good thirty years senior to his prized trophy wife, best friend of my RED. Both RED and trophy wife were not only alluring but sexy as hell. George use to love to flirt with my RED not only in front of me but also smack dab in the middle of trophy wife's vision which infuriated both of us. I think trophy wife, girl pal or not, could see her George lust for a bit of RED snapper. And what haunted her even more was that her RED might…just might fall for George's charms… he was a charming sort of guy…and that would be betrayal. And between them they could never have what they had unless everything between them, everything within them glimmered with trust. They were the closest of sisters even if they were far from being sisters in blood or law, but they enjoyed sisterhood being sister-less in real life. This was all part of their dream and also golden image that resided in their hearts. There was no room for error. There was no time for either to be seasick. There was no room for betrayal. The HEART of Truths had to be plainly played. What would turn up?

There is a saying often attributed to the late great Mayor Richard J. Daley, (da 'riginal – in Chicagoese) but I doubt he was the first to say it but whether or not that's true is irrelevant because we're talking about a fuckin' legend with a shade of pale that burned brilliantly like a star. Now what were we talkin' bout? Ah, what the Mayor said or supposedly didn't say and now I forgot. Oh yeah, "What goes around, comes around." C'mon…It's Mayor RJD, the KING of Chicago…so don't tell me I've got to dumb it down to feed the masses. And…the KING was so right because Karma has a way of correcting the course of a universe filled with assholes including a man often called an "asshole," by conclaves and tribes that made up the public and of course, his critics.

Anyway, they came clean with each other. RED let trophy wife know, as the crowd cried out for more, that her George, her fuckin' George had tried…really-really tried to mount her which clouded her shade of pale and clouded their sisterly collective shade of pale. A tear followed by a torrent of tears with a head full of RED hair in free fall embraced by a sister who deserved nothing less than complete transparency. All could be right-as-rain now between RED and trophy.

It made me feel a bit out of it. I wasn't jealous of George anymore. I was jealous of trophy wife. She had the eyes and the ears of RED in her command. I never had that, and I doubt if George ever had it with trophy wife. I take that back - partially. I don't doubt that George loved his trophy wife and even more after they had a trophy baby.

And I never doubted George's love for his daughter, Tiny Dancer. Tiny Dancer was the moniker designated before the GIT-GO by George with pure delight. I admired that about the Greek Gentleman. I let George know that one night after we had a few. I was relieved when George received my confession noting my distaste for him as the keeper of the BAR – a guy with wealth who had kept himself in remarkable shape. You never could really put a NUMBER – an age on George…I think it was the eyes. Fuck! I know it was the eyes…those CARY GRANT EYES.

When a Man Loves a Woman
After the Gig

I was still living with my parents even though I spent most of my time on the far south side of Chicago. My parents' home was on the far northwest side of the city. We had to live in the city due to my father's line of work. But I made the daily commute because I found myself in a promising band that would allow me to make some good bread playing music which I loved. And let me tell you, or you may already have heard an interview with an artiste (got to have the "e" – not the same without it) talk about how one day they were playing in a basement cubby hole of a bar and a year later picking those notes and dropping a beat on that snare drum in front of a packed house with one hundred thousand or more adoring fans.

Frankly, if we were true to our foolish pride, we wouldn't doubt a desire to announce our most fertile dreams…mine was to be a rock star. If you were halfway decent on a guitar and could play those drums…you just might wind up on MTV.

Why not it be me and *meee* bandmates? I heard that if you drop a bit of British, people in the States – notice. And I wanted to be noticed, perhaps by *meee* bandmates. That's the part that was disappointing but that only comes with time for some men…not all men and let's be forthright, men rarely get it right- anyhow! Men are a species that has severed communication challenges since Men and Women don't really communicate. And I know there's all that Dr. Phil vibe that says, "Yes, they can!" WTF. Why did everything have to be, "Si se puede?"

But as I may have alluded to, this was like the good book says, "In the Beginning." And why not let *meee* bandmates know they didn't have to worry…they didn't have a queer drummer. That sounds terrible in *hindsight* but if we all could live our lives in *hindsight*, they sure as hell wouldn't have been interesting… would they? Honestly, if everyone was perfect, life would be boring. There wouldn't be a story you could tell, not even Cinderella. You've got to have the ying & yang of good and evil because without conflict, you don't have a story. If we lose the story, we lose HI*STORY* and the Greatest Story Ever Told. That would be a tragedy. I have to have HOPE. HOPE that there is some place after the here-and-now. That may be what the doubters call a fairy tale. LOL! I love fairy tales and what lies over the rainbow.

I want to see all those I've loved and who have crossed that divide which I can't get out of my mind. When you lose a son, that kind of shit pours from your eyes, and for those who are lucky to have a confidante, it pours from your mouth as well. Sometimes the sounds are guttural because a thorn just pricked my heart. That one – that death - should never have happened during my lifetime. He should have been burying me, not the other way around. A young man with *promise*! There I go again with that word. But a father's love can't help but HOPE. In many ways he had great *promise* and not necessarily because of me. He knew what he was doing in the craft that he loved.

He loved being a DJ, the kind that brings a party of people to orgasmic frivolity, laughter and good cheer. When I now look at photos taken of my son being DJ BORAICHEE, I can't help but notice the golden glow of his smiling face, the twinkle in his eye, the *what's up* non verbiage but easily recognizable sign that comes with flailing your arms in the air or doing the epic thumbs up sign with the flashy smile. God, he was so alive!

So, here's what I know. My son had a passion for music. He also had a passion for drugs. And sometimes those two orbits can't be molded into one. Even if they could, eventually the ELEPHANT in the room would have to be addressed. Addiction? Where were we with that? But I digress from the *present* I was in when I began this chapter of the journey.

Musicians can more or less have as much liquor as they like when playing a gig. It's part of the deal. Usually when you get paid that way, you don't really make as much as you can but it was a very common practice. A club owner's biggest weekly expense then was the cost for entertainment, entertainment good enough to attract the chicks that would attract the roosters. It was *animal crackers* all over again.

If the band was any good, and ours was, then you'd have girls hitting up on you for drinks they knew you could get free of charge. And on one of my gigs, I wound up spending all my breaks with this one girl who had long, long, long blond hair, a very ample rack and smartly dressed a la Penny Lane. This girl was big boned. She wasn't fat, just big boned. She was also tall, and in her platform shoes which went with her outfit that night, she was a hair taller than me. I'd never been with a woman taller than me. I had the smug satisfaction of knowing that with our clothes off and no platform shoe influence, I would be the BIGGER of the two of us. That's all I could think about. Being BIGGER and inside of this c'est le vie woman. I couldn't help it. I was drinking way too much and so was she.

When the night came to a close, she asked me if she could crib with me. I of course said yes, even though I knew I didn't have access to a bedroom via Phil-the-Scanman. Somehow, I decided to drive home anyway with her sitting shotgun. I figured we could make it in my car. But halfway into the trip on a rather snowy and dreary Dan Ryan Expressway on a December evening in Chicago my lady of the night had literally said good night. She was slightly but noticeably snoring. All that SEX that I had envisioned with SEXY that I couldn't help but see and lust for when we were pounding them down at the club was asleep with her mouth slightly ajar. It was anything but flattering.

When we got to the driveway of my parent's home, she awoke. She looked out of the windows of my car, a bit steamy from the two of us breathing in a car that was way TOO HOT… and I'm not talking about the girl but rather the temperature of my engine. I knew I needed to replace the thermostat so that I could have more control over the surroundings. But TOO HOT seemed to enjoy the fact that she was on the other side of the city. She had never visited the Northwest side of Chicago. She wondered aloud, "And now what?"

I didn't answer. I merely pulled her close and kissed her. She kissed back and I knew we were on. I unbuckled her bra and pulled off her top. I went to start unhinging the slacks and she took her hand and put it over mine. She then grabbed my head and pushed me down to suck her breasts. I did so very willingly, every now and then coming up for air that was finished with a tender sweet kiss. She must have enjoyed that because she followed with lots of tongue. Have we had enough of the SEX one must always write into a piece of work in order to get it published? I mean, who doesn't like SEX? It's like asking, who doesn't like food? Are there two Popes? Yes, and the movie featuring Johnathan Pryce and Anthony Hopkins showcases two masters at their craft – it's that good.

But we never got passed heavy making out. I think the nap had recharged TOO HOT and with a bit of reflection, she may have reconsidered having intercourse with a complete stranger who didn't even live close to her.

I knew we couldn't stay out in the car. I was low on fuel and we would have had to run that car all night for the heat; it was snowing, and it was cold.

So, I asked TOO HOT if she'd like to come into the house. Her eyes were filled with uncertainty. I assured her that I'd find her a bed…just for her, no one else. I told her that there was no need for us to rush into something…we had just met. Maybe it was the way I said that more than what I said, because she nodded YES.

Now I had to level with her. "Look, my parents are asleep, so, we have to do this quietly."

"I knew you lived with your parents. What will they think of me?"

I started to laugh.

"What?" she said looking again like a woman TOO HOT for her own good.

"You're worried about what my parents will think? You're kidding, right?"

We both looked at one another and bust out laughing together. She looked so inviting with the smile of laughter. Her very supple ample breasts were still open to me; she had yet put on her bra or her top and so I dove once more in and she began to grind on me. We did a dry heave but before we got out of that car to sneak into that house, we both had *exploded* without worrying about anyone getting pregnant.

Decorum set in as soon as I turned that key and we entered my parents' home, my home from the fifth grade, which made me feel a bit like a fifth grader. Had I done what one of *mee* bandmates had recommended, I would have taken her to the hotel down the street and dropped part of what I made for the gig and had full on sex. She was willing before the nap, there was no mistaking that…but I fear we would have made a great mistake had we done that. I didn't have a condom, nor did she, so maybe what happened was a bit of providence. Either way, we were on a different course now. I was to serve as a shepherd and bring this fine lamb into the warmth and comfort of a bed without me in it. And so, I did just that.

My mother was up. She didn't say a word when we crossed the hallway to the stairs that lead to my bedroom. Instead she waited till I came down the steps. She handed me a pillow and a blanket for the couch in the living room. I slept alone….it was already 4 a.m. Mom suggested that I leave early before father was up. At 7, I woke up TOO HOT and shepherded her downstairs telling her to be quiet. I knew my father saw us, but I figured he wouldn't want to get into the middle of my adventure.

I took TOO HOT home that day. She lived with her parents in a neighborhood very similar to mine on the south side of Chicago, a good 30 miles away and still in the limits of the WINDY CITY. TOO HOT didn't invite me to come in to meet her parents. I didn't blame her. It was clear TOO HOT had been all night with a man – ME. And now she had to do the walk of shame even though we really hadn't done anything that either of us had to worry about. How come there never was a walk of shame for men? Actually, I did get a very salty look thrown my way by a man staring out the bay window as I helped TOO HOT out of the car. She was suffering from either a really bad hangover or dizziness from not having a good night's rest.

TOO HOT didn't kiss me goodbye or even ask if I was going to call? How could I? She never gave me her number. It was good that we didn't go farther. I would have enjoyed seeing her, but we never did. And to think we could have conceived someone in the heat of our lust, the heat of our passion and for what? A lot of heartache, and a shade of pale that hurts.

Could we have fallen in love? A fairy tale love?

I'm not sure.

But then we never got the chance to find out.

A Man Among Men Worth Loving

My dad was a fireman. He lived and breathed being a first responder. He loved being a firefighter which wasn't a mere job, it was a passion.

Whenever and wherever we'd go on a vacation, which was all done with a wife riding shotgun and three kids climbing over each other in the back seat of a Plymouth – we would have to stop at the local fire department station. It didn't matter if it was a hick town in Alabama or a large city like D.C. …there we were, our green Plymouth parked next to the apron of a fire station waiting for dad to return from meeting his brothers-in-arms. And it didn't matter that he was a northerner when we were in the deep, deep South. That's where we ate black-eye peas and grits…actually none of us kids ate the grits, but they were fun to look at and play with.

Dad was a smoke eater – a firefighter – and it didn't matter when we were in the South that he was a Northerner. Maybe if we had been BLACK the reception might not have been so congenial, since we traveled at a time when the CROW named JIM flew. But, I'm not even sure that would have mattered. If dad had been BLACK, they might not have wanted him on their department, but I think they'd understand that in the North, people of color sometimes were given jobs that only a person with a whiter shade of pale could expect to hold in a hamlet in Mississippi. But that was never an issue since we were white. I learned a lot on that road trip as our automobile roared through the dusty roads of Kentucky, Tennessee, Mississippi, Louisiana, Alabama, Georgia and then onto sunny Florida. I learned that the USA was united, but oh so different from state to state. And yet, somehow, we remained unified; upon reflection and age like the time it takes to make a fine wine, I now know why.

All adults, black or white, were united that America would always rule itself and never have to endure again the nightmare of a lunatic like Hitler serving as a potential master. It was still fresh in the minds of most of the adults which even me and my siblings knew. Our block was identical in some ways because the war had been a stamp as deep as any found on the arm of a Holocaust survivor. Americans were enjoying the benefits of peace – at least white Americans were. We had nice things, a home with a Grandma attached to it, and a car which some couldn't afford. We were right there in the middle of middle class.

And we had that which a lot of other kids didn't have. We had parents who liked to travel even if it meant having to make those rides with three kids playing war games in the back seat of a sedan. When we returned on that trip, FATHER FIRE-FIGHTER, took a whole new route on the return to the North. We saw bits and pieces of Georgia upon leaving Florida and then cut through South & North Carolina with a swing through Virginia, West Virginia, Ohio, north for a few miles to Michigan and then south to Indiana on our way into Chicago. We saw a lot from ground zero and not in some airplane at 36,000 feet. We caught the smells of the local cuisine…hell, that's too fine a word for what I'm trying to say. Each locale had its own shade of pale, shade of aroma, shade of scent often colored by the food indigenous to the natives. Gumbos, soups, barbeque, grits, black-eye peas, venison, shellfish, mushrooms, tomatoes, vineyard grapes, and spices awoke me to the fact that food could be not only interesting but exciting - a lot more than just Chicago hot dogs and pizza, which are America's finest! My mother and father gave me that. My mother didn't know how to drive, so my father drove all those miles. I could be off a bit, but I think we traveled some 3,000 miles and saw a significant portion of our United States.

The following year, a trip to the East Coast included numerous states that were not covered in the Florida trip. That trip East included stops in D.C. Philly, NY and then north into New England. By the time I was ten, I had visited some 26 states, or a little more than half of the United States. I share this timeline in honor of my FATHER FIREFIGHTER who wanted his family on the salary of a fireman to see the beauty of America. I say America because on the return trip back from East to Midwest Chicago we took a detour north to Montreal. You didn't need a passport then to travel from the U.S. to the land of the Maple Leaf's.

And with that diversion, I had racked up a country. I could brag when I returned from summer vacation to my school mates that I had…yes, little old me, had been outside of the United States of America. I found that exhilarating. I wish I still had that kind of *esprit de corps*.

I had a love/hate relationship with FATHER FIRE-FIGHTER (FF).

He could be so stubborn. So, could I.

He could be so sensitive. So, could I.

He could be so much fun. So, could I.

He could be so real. So…hmmm, that's a tough one.

We were each other's image, only with a number of years in between the bookends. We had the same look which was much more imprinted than in either of my siblings, but especially more than the oldest male, which I wasn't. That just shouldn't have been, but it was.

The oldest male looked more like mother.

And so, we were up in each other's craw, all the time. It was like a game we played. In every family, there are definitive lines of demarcation on who does what and who doesn't. I wasn't having any of that and so we, FF & I, knocked heads frequently. I should have been knocked out, but I wasn't. I gave as good as I got.

But I found the man at times when I was sporting a crummy shade of pale open to talking.

There are two moments I will never forget between my FATHER FIREFIGHTER and me...may I please be a bit uncouth and insist that it be between FATHER FIRE-FIGHTER and EYE? Yes, I know it should read *FF and I (actually me)*. BUT you do have to admit, that if you have one's EYE, you have one's attention.

Let me recall them as they occurred.

The first one made quite the impression in my mini-mind, because it happened when I was so, very, very young – a mere shade of pale that had just turned three. Maybe I saw it when I actually found myself floating above the crowd that had min-gled around my body, struck down by a teenage driver driving way too fast on a residential street with kids. I was feeling a wee bit seasick. And there HE was...out of nowhere returning from the grocery store in that green Plymouth that would later take us across half of the U.S.A. He had to pull up because of a crowd gathered around something in the middle of the street. What was it? What are they looking at? The questions irked him and so he exited that green Plymouth, to find out that some-times being home isn't all that it's cracked up to be.

He saw his son lying flat on the street - lifeless. He cried out, "Move away…move away…that's my son!" FF did what he had been trained to do as a fireman. He got his son, carried him, sans car, to the hospital at the end of the block.

The son was taken into an operating theater. The doctors huddled over him as the room hummed courtesy of the overhead lights…it was a theater of sorts. Anyway, they looked him up and down and then one of them said, "His eyes are open. He must be okay." At least that's what I thought I heard from my drifting above in a white shade of clouds. I then found myself sinking, sinking, sinking…which meant I had to return to earth as I gasped for air and somehow came back to life. Maybe the word resurrected might be a better way to describe it. That moment was the here and now of being alive in a world of sinners.

The other moment…I will always carry in my heart. IT was an emotional side of my FATHER FIREFIGHTER and me that we rarely ever found together. I was feeling kind of seasick again when I sought out the man shortly after he had come home from work. It was a weekend and so I was up early when the man of smoke walked into our home. You couldn't help but notice the musty smell in the clothes, in the hair. I didn't care. I needed to talk.

I asked if we could talk.

I had taken my entrance exam at a high school known as Quigley Seminary for Boys. I did that purely from suffering obsessive compulsive disorder induced by a brain washing inflicted upon me at a very tender age, that I…I was the one… the one who would be given to the Church in hopes that son #1 became a hit in life. That sounds more cynical or maybe pathetic than even I could have imagined.

I believe an alien force has taken control of my fingers pounding out the script we now find ourselves mired in.

But the bottom line was that I didn't want to go. I didn't want to be a priest even though it had been drummed into me that I would be the chosen one. To my surprise and maybe my good fortune, my FATHER FIREFIGHTER said, "Then you shouldn't go there. Now you needn't get upset." I'm not sure my mother who was far more religious than PA-PA would have dismissed the matter so quickly. I would have had to endure a bit more guilt before mother would let it go. She had her own side deals going with Mother Mary and I think I may have been one of them. Sorry to disappoint MOM, but hey – it was my life – right?

I was afraid I wouldn't be able to get into my brother's parochial high school. Before I came out of the closet and revealed that I wasn't gay and therefore had no interest in the priesthood, I had shared with friends but not family, that I had wanted to go to that high school filled with bulldogs (the school's mascot).

Why did I allow myself to be led like that? I was certain it would be impossible to reverse the run-away-train I found myself on - or so I thought.

FF was so calm that I couldn't help but take in a deep breath and reduce my boiling blood pressure to normal. He had this. He had assured me he would fix it.

I'll never forget when he put his arm around me as we both sat on the edge of my bed while I sobbed crying out that I just didn't want to become a man of the cloth. I had other ideas and my recurring dream always had me ending up with *The Red-Haired Woman*. That didn't jive with being celibate, a foul, foul, dirty word in my brain.

After my confession, FF put on his fire captain uniform and made a trip to see the parochial high school principal.

I don't know what he said or how he made it happen and frankly I didn't care. All that mattered was that FF did it. I went to that lucky canine charm of a parochial school in the shadow of son #1 who was quite the valedictorian.

Those two moments in time always fill me with a brighter shade of pale about my father and my life.

So, those of us who are lucky are blessed with men in their lives that guide them, teach them and grant them the ability to live a life with a Casper the ghostly shade of pale. That's why men like me never forget what a father gives out of love. You don't necessarily get a lot of hugs and touchy-feely-stuff, but you lose your seasickness because you know that with father next to you in your life, any dream you have could be possible. A man like FF can give you the sea legs you need to make your journey come true.

If that ain't LOVE than I don't know what is?

The Older Woman

For the LEWD, this will be a disappointment.

I met the older woman when I was a mere 17. I was a paper boy. Being a paper boy is a concept that must be explained, just as one might do with a T-REX exhibit. Paper boys would literally drop a morning or an afternoon or a late edition of the daily newspaper on your doorstep. If you were a kid and you wanted to make some money with your bike, being a paper boy was a coveted job in the teen set. At that time, newspapers were still king in the world of media.

I'll put my older woman somewhere around 47 – or about 30 years my senior. During the Spring, Summer and Fall months, 47 would sit on her stoop, smoking a cigarette, waiting for that delivery. Maybe she was a writer who wrote something in that edition or a news junkie as my father like to call them.

I literally handed 47 the paper I was delivering. She snatched at it with her finely manicured talons. I stepped away when I heard, "Hey, what's your name. I should know the name of my paper delivery boy."

I couldn't help but squint with shame when I heard the OY ring of the word, "boy," which deflated the pride of a young 17-year-old man.

But I found myself compelled to answer. "My name…my name is Sidney. You can call me Sid." I had no intention of giving that woman my real name, so for now, the closest she got was the nomenclature of my pup.

"Well, Sid or is it Sidney?"

"Either works," I said.

She smiled at me and I took her in. To my surprise, she was remarkably attractive. Good figure, pretty face, blonde hair, and dressed smartly if not a bit provocatively.

"Well, Sid, could you make sure that I also get the Sunday edition as well?"

"If you can give me a phone number, I can make sure that I have a subscription specialist call you."

She smiled at me. 47 had a pink shade of pale shorts that showed off two very fine legs. 47 looked like she had inherited Betty Grable's gams, immortalized and made famous during the war that followed the war to end all wars.

I had seen enough Bogie films to know what the *look* was – between Humphrey and Lauren Bacall. 47 shot my heart with that *look*.

"You look thirsty. Would you like to come in for a glass of Lemonade? It's cold – and - it's tart but kissed with just the right amount of sweet to make you wanting even more."

I might have been only 17 at the time but I was no dummy. This woman – this 47 – intrigued me. I could spend 15 minutes to have a drink and still get all my papers delivered. I was that naïve.

And that's how it started. The myth, the promise of the fairy tale was kept.

47 wanted companionship. That was it. 47 wanted to talk to someone who would listen. It was obvious that the men in 47's life didn't appreciate the charm of this woman. I'm not sure what 47 did for money, for the bills, but it was clear she did not lack for

anything. Her flat was beautifully decorated and she had a bar, fully locked and loaded tucked into a cute corner next to the fireplace.

I'm not sure if I lusted for 47 but curiosity got the better of me and I yearned to be with a femme fatale that fascinated me. I had recently seen the movie, "Summer of '42," with creamy, dreamy Jennifer O'Neill as Dorothy the older woman who helped men my age season. "Summer of '42," captured the Oscar for Best Picture. I wanted to live one of those roles; 47 had a sex appeal that was hopelessly appealing. Like a virgin I craved carnal knowledge bestowed on me, by a saucy but sensuous 47.

I've had a lot of birthday parties, but I have forgotten more than I remember. But I'll never forget my 18th birthday. 47 made me a chocolate cake to celebrate. I knew something was UP, besides my penis which was constantly in a state of hard-on. Something was very different in how 47 brushed against me while serving me that chocolate delight and then squeezed into me on the bench of that picnic table that sat inside her house. Yeah, I know. It was weird but that was 47. I could tell from the way she put her hand on my back while I was lapping up the cream from the vanilla that melted on the chocolate cake that was so moist, so wet, that I thought I might fall into a pool of cum. And I did.

After the cake, the room with that picnic table grew hotter and hotter. 47 grabbed the back of my skull and gently, oh so gently pulled me into her moist red lips. I went from a white shade of pale to that of a crimson, crimson, RED shade of pale as my oxygenated dick would not let me be without my tongue in her mouth and me giving her a slurpee. Wow…that's a bit more descriptive than I wanted to share, but IT was ON!

IT went on and on all night. When the morning came, I got a nice gentle kiss goodbye and a look that said, "We're not doing what we did last night, ever again!"

I wasn't mad. I was disappointed. I enjoyed the evening and would have liked to reprise the SEX again. It was kind of cool to be with an older, more experienced woman. She could expand a young man's horizon, which was what she did for me. And the SEX was amazing…the shade of pale on that was nothing less than stellar…absolutely stellar. Ah shit! I was mad. Why did she BLUE BALL me like that. Come on, she wasn't married, nor was I and hell, we did dig being with one another. That was due in part to the fact that we had talked for that year about everything and anything before I became legal. All that conversation helped us find one another on a level that was A-sexual. Maybe being A-sexual wasn't so bad after all.

I got to know 47.

47 had quite a story. She had been in the camps; you know the death camps in NAZI controlled Europe. I can't remember now, which camp it was or even why her family got rounded up…they weren't Jewish. Maybe, and this is me making a con-jecture…they had been part of the *resistance*? I was young but I knew about the *resistance* because I loved reading history.

47 told me how she and her mother survived a father shot in the head by an SS officer trying to make a point when the boxcars unloaded.

47's life was anything but a soft shade of pale.

I would have liked to just go back and be a part of that A-sexual life with 47…because in my mind the room got hotter and hotter just uncovering the woman. I wanted to know this woman. I didn't expect to know her carnally even though it hap-pened to my surprise. The images of that evening are embedded in the neurons of my brain. It was wild. It was fun. It was tender. It was soothing. It was a whiter shade of pale than I 'd ever expected.

So, yeah, I was crest fallen. Why didn't 47, permit me to learn more, much more about love and lust and why that twain could or maybe - never - should meet?

Whenever I dug deep into my past, I couldn't help but remember 47 and what she gave a young gangling boy seeking his right of passage to become a man. Just the thought of 47 brought me bliss. I can't say the same for some of the women in my life but for 47, I can always find a blissful smile.

The Virgin Mary

They were both young, but the man was a good eight years older. He was working for a television network and she was at a medium size market station in Missouri. They wound up sitting next to each other at the keynote address of an annual convention attended by professionals in the marketing world of television promotion.

She was a looker who could rock a business suit with slacks and could easily have been in front of the camera rather than behind it. Blond hair with long bangs, blue eyes, a cute figure with a great rack and a smile that revealed a set of dazzling teeth… all part of the young woman's arsenal of attributes. He was tall, handsome, athletically built and had the confidence that comes with a man who has made a name for himself in his field of endeavor. He was *confident man.*

Their sexual attraction to one another was so palpable that you could cook with it. And yet, it was complicated. He had a ring on his finger and so did she. As they found out, neither were in viable relationships. His ring was tarnished by a separation that was dissolving into divorce. She wore her cheesy ruby ring to ward off men…she just wasn't in the right shade of pale to deal with one at the moment. At least that's what she told herself.

They caught the seminars together. She was always nattily dressed in a pants suit and he in his three-piece. They ate together and after the day's festivities drank vodka tonics next to a pool that kept everyone in a very hot state, cool. They were definitely in a hot state of anxiety besides enjoying the beams that soaked the Land of Enchantment — New Mexico. It was so obvious that what they wanted was to sleep together and yet that didn't happen until the last day before they were to depart the convention. Even then it almost didn't happen.

She had invited him back to her hotel room during the middle of the last day…during the middle of the seminars. She told him she needed to talk with him privately. He wasn't sure what to expect. Despite his solitude and self-imposed abstinence from intercourse with female companionship due in part to confusion…the kind of confusion one encounters when a kindred soul dies in one's heart, he wanted to find out what she had to share.

There was a part of that very *confident* man that was anything but *confident* when it came to his feelings for his soon-to-be ex-wife. But when you know something is dead, you're a drunk crazy for a drink in the middle of a storm hoping that something magical will be born and all your troubles are healed.

They sat on the edge of the bed. She had a photo album next to her that she grabbed and opened for *confident man* to see. It showed her in a number of photos with friends, male and female, sporting a hair-do that featured long, long blonde curls, pulled back into a pony-tail and bang-less, unlike her current hair-do, which was short on the sides and the back with long bangs that covered her entire forehead.

She broke the silence. "I have never been with a man."

He wasn't sure how to react to such a confession other than find himself in a bit of shock. How does a beautiful woman sitting next to him remain a virgin into her early twenties? He said nothing and waited.

"Let me show you something." She threw the photo album behind her onto the pillows. She grabbed a sweat band from out of nowhere that had a logo of the St. Louis Cardinals sewn into it with the words, "Go CARDS." She was a Missourian. The sweat band was placed over her head so she could pull back the bangs to reveal a hideous looking scar that she had done a great job of hiding with Max Factor and a coif that was smart.

"How'd that happen?" *Confident man* didn't have a clue on how to react. Maybe a question wouldn't seem insensitive?

"I was in an accident, when I was 16. I'm not sure how my head got scarred but that was the least of my problems. I lost my left leg from my knee down."

Confident man put his arm around the woman. "I'm sorry to hear you went through all of that Mary. I'd never have known if you hadn't told me." Maybe that made me like a lot of men, dotards who failed to notice what's right in front of them.

Silence reigned for a good thirty seconds.

Mary exhaled a deep breath. "That's why I've never been with a man."

Confident man cocked his head to the right and then said, "I'm sorry to hear that as well."

"I don't want you feeling sorry for me. What I want, or at least what I think I want is a night of passion. We literally spend the rest of our last day and night in this room…with you making love, tenderly to me. Can you do that?"

Confident man flashed her a red-blooded American smile, "Sure."

"Can you really?" Her tone was confrontational. "Because a woman with a stump and a scarred face might be a bit too much for a handsome fellow like you. So please, think about this carefully. Can you make me feel like a woman who is wanted, who is lusted despite her physical deformities? If you can't, I promise I won't judge you badly for that."

Confident man didn't respond with words. He used his hands to caress her face and then gave her long wet kisses. Gently, very gently he undressed her and viewed an ample perky bosom.

"Stop!"

He stopped.

"I'm not sure I can do this. I feel like such a tease. I didn't mean to do that. Please don't be angry." She held her eyes low before making contact with the man sitting next to her.

Confident man looked deep into her eyes and mouthed the words without vocalizing them, *It's okay* - over and over. In a soft voice he said, "Mary, your first should be very special…maybe someone you love, and I mean lovvvvvve."

She merely nodded. He got up to leave when she grabbed his hand, pulled him back and placed his hand on her breast. She then arose from the bed and kissed her visitor gently on each cheek, on his nose, on his forehead and finally on his lips.

They danced back to the bed and both fell upon it as they tore off clothes and *Confident man,* made tender love to Mary despite the torrential rain of tears that inundated his soul. There was nothing about the woman that turned him off. He kissed the scar on her face and as he traveled down the highway of her body to her wet spot, he made it a point to kiss the stump. He made it a point to move slowly and didn't want her ever to recover from the intensity of his lovemaking. When he entered her, he did it ever so gently but as the passion rose, he gave her what she wanted, tenderness.

It was only when they gave it another go that she wanted him to give her a royal fuck that she'd always remember. It was her first time experiencing the carnal appetite of a man and she was from the show-me-state and she wanted to be shown and he did better than good…he did it royally just the way she wanted it.

When they departed the next day, she insisted that they take a photo together in front of a fountain that bubbled in their hotel lobby. She had one of those little ten shot cameras that drug stores used to sell long ago. She was wearing a long summer dress that almost touched the floor; a dress splashed with yellow gold patterns that bounced light onto her face that made her look ebullient.

They both smiled because that's what you do in photos, even if you know that the one, you're taking the photo with, might never be in your life again. Behind those glistening eyes were thoughts.

Confident man figured he'd eventually wind up in Mary's photo album. He was her first and for that reason if no other he was sure she wanted a remembrance of the man who helped her blossom and vanquish the albatross of virginity.

Her thoughts were that of a conqueror. She had bagged a man. She had arrived and was finally a female seductress. At least that's what she told herself.

They both knew they were ships passing in the night off to a shade of pale where ships like them eventually go to die. But for that one-small-moment, they would always have each other in the Land of Enchantment, friends first, then lovers, then fuckers and only after all that, as ships passing in the night.

Inadvertently they had helped themselves by helping the other.

For that speck in time, they enjoyed bliss, the bliss that comes from the tenderness that fills a heart hurting from rejection, be it imposed or inflicted.

Moon Over Miami

"Did I ever tell you, Delilah, that the SEX was….hmmm, how should I put this? ORGASMIC….hmm, hmm, hmm uh…. girl, that man could get me OFF!" Sheryl was chilling, having a glass of Cabernet, she loved wine…that's kind of how she met the man who made her trip to Miami so magical.

Little did either of the Miami moon glow lovers know they were going to be paramours when they got on that plane, to leave Chicago for the sunny limes of Florida and that incredible Key-lime pie made delectable by that tart but luscious carnal piece of fruit. Sheryl hadn't been with a man for over two years and frankly, it didn't bother her. Most of the men she met were on the hunt, married but very much inclined to do a bit of mating even though their mates were twelve hundred miles away.

But were they really AWAY? None of those possible trysts would ever lead to something substantial…it didn't have to be BIG…it just had to BE…like EXCLUSIVE? How can one ever have that while the other has a GK – a Gordian Knot - on the finger next to the little finger on the left hand, on which the GK is worn. Men were so brazen since the commencement of the era of drumpf, that a woman had best abandon men for a vibrator, which in many cases was a lot more satisfying.

Delilah chuckled devilishly. "I know all about that girl. Must you carry on so? It sometimes makes me WET!"

Both women BUST out laughing; the kind of infectious laugh that goes on and on and then when you think it's going to lay down and die - it ERUPTS again like that old friendly Geyser out in Yellowstone. Actually, that kind of laughter is good for the soul and the body.

"Oh, c'mon, you love when I tell the tale. Are you sipping some wine?"

Delilah grabbed her glass of White Chablis and took a sip. "I am now honey."

So, Sheryl started. The one good thing Delilah always appreciated, was that when Sheryl told her prince charming story, she always changed it up a bit. Delilah loved to catch the changes because they told her something about her BFF – Best Friend Forever.

Sheryl and Delilah were BFFs – Best Friends Forever.

They had met while working on the Oprah Winfrey Show and the one thing they always agreed on was that Oprah had been a Godsend for both of them. Working on that show as associate producers was a trip. Oprah was a trip. The money was a trip. The guests were a trip. The perks were a trip.

It was a dream job.

But it also was a BURNOUT position. The hours could be all-consuming. The show was #1. There's only one way you keep that. YOU EARN IT.

And so, Delilah went back to school to become a CHEF and Sheryl somehow swung a pretty nice gig with WTTW, the public television powerhouse in Chicago. When Sheryl was there, it was often known for being the best watched PBS station in America – per capita.

After Sheryl left WTTW and became an executive with a major health care provider, she didn't think much about her days at Channel 11 (as it's known in Chicago) until about ten years later when she got an invitation to go to a WTTW reunion for a weekend in Miami. The price was reasonable. The group rate factor applied; the airfare was provided at a nominal charge (taxes only) by the Chicago based major airline carrier that literally loved their underwriting status and support of WTTW. It made them good corporate citizens. Everyone loved Mr. Rogers, BIG BIRD and company on PBS, and people loved the carrier for being so supportive. In those days, whatever was good for the kids was sublime.

"And there he was standing next to me at the bar and he said, 'Hi there. Can I get you a Cabernet?' It was as if he took one look at me and knew I loved red wine."

Both women took a wine-sipping break if only for a moment.

"I was surprised. What was this white guy doing? He was asking me, a woman of color if he could buy me a drink. I couldn't help but think Dee, if he was just being polite or he was very lonely."

"Don't ever say that! How many times have I told you Sheryl, to never say that?"

"Oh please! I know I'm a catch. And being half African, half French, perhaps even a bit EXOTIC. But you don't understand. WTTW was a place that was very buttoned up – in some ways very British. All of that Masterpiece Theater shit must have rubbed off on those people. There was a reason why people said, 'The call letters WTTW stand for Wilmette talks to Winnetka, two very white and wealthy North Shore enclaves.' However, it's funny. I don't remember him when he worked at WTTW. It was a big place. There were over 500 employees."

"I know Sheryl, I've heard all that. Get to the good part so I can COME," Delilah coughed impishly, "COME to know your happy ending."

That's when more laughter erupted. It was almost as if they had smoked a BONG dry which they couldn't have, since they were only connected on this night by cellular waves. Well, maybe they could have but it didn't matter, they each had their WINE and that was more than enough to do the trick. But one of the concerns was that the incessant laughter might cause one of them or both of them a STROKE of good luck…that their next sexual encounter could be as good as the one that broke a bed…it was that HARD of a ride; that long ride they enjoyed under the Moon of Miami.

"The ride turned into a love affair. He was recently divorced with two girls, two very protective girls and it had nothing to do with my skin color. The man was awash in tears at times over his girls. And me, Dee, having two girls, I could relate. He did not hesitate to show me off to his friends. He was so comfortable with me being African as I was comfortable with him being so ITALIAN – so VERY WHITE even with the olive glow."

Sheryl needed a taste of the grape before she continued.

"After our meeting in Miami, we returned without all the racket. It was just the two of us. We left bitter cold to immediately feel the beat of that SUN on the beach…and then I felt the BEAT of his stroke….it was languid, so relaxed that I wondered why the soft touch? I was used to HARD and I lusted for it… but something about this disinclination for physical exertion was novel. I was feeling a SWELL move over me like the waves you find that the surfers love to tunnel through. SWELL after SWELL engulfed me. I was as WET as WET could be. I turned such a white shade of pale which made my mulatto coloring blossom into a shade of rich, rich cocoa chocolate that dripped of sweat caused not by exertion but by the longing for that hypnotic stroke. If this was heaven, then - Hallelujah. I'd made it to the promised land. Oh, Delilah, the man felt soooooooooo

GOOD. And yet, I knew I was soooooo BAD. I couldn't help but wonder why a grown woman like me didn't exact more of a commitment from my slice of WHITE IVORY. After all, I was a church-going woman."

"Praise the Lord…she is a good woman Messiah!" Delilah's voice rang out over those radio waves hoping that the Lord himself would tune in to their conversation.

"When he wouldn't give me that, I tumbled. It was my own fault."

"Don't say that Sheryl. Why you saying that girl? Don't do that!"

"I never told you the truth. So tonight, I'm confessing to my BFF."

"Is this a trick twist just to keep me interested?" Delilah took a sip of her wine waiting.

"No trick. I just couldn't admit it." Sheryl swirled her Chablis as it turned a brighter shade of pale. "He told me he wasn't going to marry again. As he put it, 'We've both done it, have the T-Shirt and really don't need to do that again. But what I will give you is my heart and along with that you are the only one I enter. That's a promise on the life of my girls, and you know I'd never say that if I didn't mean it.'"

"BUT what always got me Dee, he'd say ENTER just as he was entering. Oh my! That certainly gave me that rich cocoa brown shade of pale that was/is so alluring."

"Oh my! I think I'm going to have to change my panties before I lay down tonight." An impish cough followed by the one and only Delilah.

"I'm glad you're enjoying this, Dee." Sheryl took a sip. "I didn't know how to end it, so, I left it to him to figure it out and confront me. He knew my frequent headaches were my way of keeping him from entering and yet I wanted him to enter me over and over and over and over again. It felt that rich."

"I told you girl! You were a fool not to compromise with the man on that. You have never ever shared with me since you two moved on - the kind of buzz you got from anyone else compared to that love. When we're together and across from one another, I see it in your eyes. I hear it in your voice. I sense the dimples in your skin when you mention his name. I think you feel a bit seasick without the love of that man."

"I do. He gave me confidence. He loved the way I looked, and he didn't hesitate to tell me or show me how much. But it did lead me to get engaged again with a very fine man."

"Uh…huh. A very fine man nowhere near as fine as that fine man who made you experience a heavenly shade of pale… not bad for a black bitch." That's how they always ended the conversation. Delilah loved to call her BFF a 'black bitch.' She was a slice of EBONY and proud of it, so, Sheryl never took offense at how Dee ended her stream of consciousness.

It was one of those romances that still allowed both Sheryl and her lover to get together now and then for a drink and take in a bit of jazz. Sheryl eventually dropped the fiancé who wasn't nearly as fine as that WHITE man with the olive glow. It just didn't feel right in the end.

When they came together, they would talk and talk. They were so easy together. They laughed and laughed. They held hands and at the end of the night, they even kissed; it was always a sweet gentle blissful kiss.

A sure sign that ensured they'd never-ever-again break the bed.

Missing

They met while walking through the cafeteria line at the WTTW/ PBS building in Chicago. They both had grabbed a salad.

She was tall but very feminine. Liz had a face you might see in a painting by a classic artist like Leonardo da Vinci featuring a spirit with big bluer than blue eyes, jet black hair that traveled down her back and caressed her very fine looking ass and a pair of legs that went on and on after the skirt gave up trying to cover them. The white satin blouse she filled out so curvedly, reflected the light from Mr. Sun that entered a very fancy cafeteria through a wall of windows that looked onto a rose garden. No matter what they tell you, public television had its perks.

He was a wee bit taller than her and dressed very GQ with a glen plaid green double-breasted vest, subtle but elegant. His brown hair had enough red in it that it went well with the freckles on his face. His features were spooky in how young they made him look, but his big brown eyes exuded with the experience one might expect from a life of 38 years.

Both could turn a head and together they were simply quite smashing.

She began the dance just as she checked out. "Oh, I see, you're having a salad just like mine. Well, it must be good then. This is my first day at WTTW."

Mr. Plaid smiled. "Actually, everything here is good. And they subsidize the cost, so eat up…and yeah, the Cobb isn't bad. May I join you?"

Mona was surprised by the cashier's interruption, "That'll be two dollars please Miss." Upon giving up a $2.00 bill, the cashier chuckled, "Well somebody's been to the track." Mona smiled and said to Mr. Plaid, "Wow you weren't kidding about subsidizing."

Mr. Plaid grinned impishly. "Oh, I'd never kid about something like that." He then looked at her as he cocked his head from left to right to say without saying it, "So, am I joining you or not?"

Mona must have felt it and said, "Why, of course, yes, please join me. But I must tell you that I'll pick your brain for sure on how this place works."

He nodded and then lead her to a corner table where they might enjoy some privacy.

She was at WTTW to work on a project as an associate producer on a special being produced for PBS about the world of cinema. Roger Ebert and Gene Siskel, hosts of the very popular film critique show, *SNEAK PREVIEWS*, also produced by WTTW would serve as writers and narrators for the special.

Her being at WTTW was a sheer fluke. While serving as a diplomatic attaché, she made friends with an on-location manager for a feature film. That friendship with the newfound gal-pal, who also served as a freelance TV producer was how Mona wound up at PBS. It's always connections when it comes to opportunity. That TV assignment as an associate producer would secure for Mona about 12 weeks of employment, a blessing in light of her decision to take an unpaid three-month sabbatical from the State Department. Chicago was home for Mona. Her parents, who had not seen her for more than three years were thrilled to have her stay at their home.

"So, what was the movie?" Mr. Plaid was a bit of a movie buff. "Missing." She took a fork full of salad as if to let her answer sink in. He seemed puzzled.

"Missing? Was that the one with Jack Lemmon and Sissy Spacek?"

"Yes, that's it. The one about…

"Chile? The military coup?"

She smiled a YES. They were already finishing each other's sentences. The last time Mona found herself immersed in a man who could do that, he broke her heart.

"So, this is a story I want to hear. How did you wind up in the movie…how about we go to dinner tonight, my treat, and you share that with me?"

"We haven't even finished our salads and you're asking me out on a date?" She smiled but with a lip turned down. "How about we stick to lunch for now?"

Mr. Plaid wasn't sure how to reply, so he didn't which left on the table a platter of SILENCE.

"Look, I only go out with men who are single."

"Well, then we don't have a problem."

"But your ring?"

"Ah, my ring. Yes, that was my father's. He gave it to me on his death bed."

"Oh, I am so sorry. I…I

"It's okay. Truth be told, I am separated and have been for quite some time. I live by myself, but I do have two young daughters, one that's nine and the other one is five. Frankly, I haven't been out to dinner with a woman on a date in over two years, but that's no reason why you should go out with me."

She looked down at her salad. The room had suddenly got smaller.

"I've got to get back. But maybe we could have lunch tomorrow, same time?"

That was the hope he needed.

"I'll actually have more time." The blue eyes were inviting.

He didn't need her to give him a reason WHY she had appeared reluctant. He felt stupid. He had come off like a smooth operator, the farthest thing from a man who had been celibate for two years. But he had. That *part* was very real, very lonely. *Part* of that loneliness had been self-imposed. He just wasn't interested in that *part of life, the part* of *life* where you literally put your heart beat on your sleeve, only to find that *part of your life* was not as it seems; the dream of the sweet intoxication of love turns to rain and empty skies above and it's nothing but SHIT.

He really did want to hear her story.

The next day they tried the Chinese with shrimp. It was a coincidence. He was already seated at that same table when she ordered and cashed out. She arrived to hear an enthusiastic confirmation.

"You got a good one!"

Mona smiled when she noticed he had the same. As she took her seat Mr. Sun hit her just so and her ivory blouse reflected onto a face that blossomed with a wondrous shade of pale.

"So how about that story?" Ask and you shall receive Mr. Plaid.

"The story? Oh, yeah. But wasn't that the one you wanted to hear over dinner?"

They both laughed knowing that a DATE had been set.

Mr. Plaid picked a small neighborhood restaurant in the Logan Square area of the city which had an amazing chef, who had yet to come to the attention of the food critics of either the

Sun-Times or the Tribune and thus still afforded an opportunity for an intimate dinner.

Mona had been working as a diplomat for the State Department. She was burned out after working in Cameroon, where her so-so French became magnifique. She grew tired of every man, Cameroon, French or American offering nothing more than the sweet intoxication of LOVE.

She decided she needed a break from State and wound up on a lark attending an audition call at an off-Broadway theater while accompanying her brother Steven in New York, who she had come to visit for a few days. Steven was a struggling actor with a few bright highlights and hope based on a Yale degree in acting. He would go on one day to be quite the character actor with quite the resume, but on this day, he did not impress the director, quirky renown French-Greek Costas Gavras, who often cast non-actors, hoping to achieve authenticity of character for minor roles. Costas spotted Mona and approached her.

"Are you an actress?" Mona's brother Steven was standing next to Costas. The look between siblings was priceless. Steven was not aware at that specific moment in time and space that he hadn't got the part of FRANK. So, his eyes dramatically appealed to his sister to not fuck up how she dealt with CG.

Mona knew exactly how to handle this minefield. She gave CG quite the smile and then chuckled slowly building the chuckle into a soft laugh that grew orgasmic-ALLY (and make sure you put some emphasis on the ALLY) into a one-of- a-kind moment in the universe of laughter that was nothing less than a massive volcanic eruption into uncontrollable hysteria. CG laughed and so did her brother…and it wasn't a fake sort of laugh. Steven had been convinced of his sister's ability to act. After all, didn't Shakespeare once say, "All the world's a stage and all the men and women merely players." The difference between Mona and her brother Steven, when it came to acting was that Mona plied her craft in real life conditions. It was Mona who had stared down a guy in Cameroon brandishing an UZI as a local militia tried to intimidate the denizens of the U.S. embassy...had Steven been involved, it would have been on a set in NY or Hollywood...big difference. So, Mona was more than adept at reading the situation, analyzing a course of action and then executing without any equivocation or as a commercial popular at that time noted that, "Whatever you do, don't let them see you sweat!"

When the laughter finally subsided, it was Costa who began to act.

"Let me guess what you do besides being ravishing. Even my wife would approve."

Steven and Mona smiled at that one. That's when her dear brother deigned to introduce her to the Maestro.

"Costa, this is my sister-

"You don't think I know it's your sister?' Costa gave Steven a quirky but somewhat mild and yet to the point rebuff of a smile.

"Mona, may I introduce you to the director of the upcoming film, "MISSING?"

Mona was hesitant to get involved in their intramural fire. She replied in French, sure that someone as worldly as Gavras would appreciate.

"Enchante Monsieur Gavras."

"Le plaisir est pour moi (the pleasure is mine), mademoi-selle. Call me Costa." The big man served up a welcoming serve.

"Ok, Costa."

"Let me guess what you do?"

Steven was amazed and asked, "What?"

"Steven, if you don't mind, I'm trying to have a conversation with your sister, Mona. Could you afford us a little...space?"

Steven nodded. "I'll be near by sis." He turned and walked away giving into CG. He was frankly interested in knowing what he was proposing to his sister. It's funny. He never really appreciated her beauty until another man, a strange quirky man who had known Mona for no more than two minutes saw her as a dish but also as a possible actor for his upcoming film. That was Gavras' thing – and what a thing it was.

"Now back to what it is you do. I see you in an executive position doing something dealing with negotiation…the art of the deal as some might call it."

Mona's lips parted and the whites of her teeth, a beautiful set of ivory, sparkled back at Gavras. "Not bad…you're on it just not in it."

"Yet." Costa's lips were together, but you could see the twinkle in the man's eyes.

"Would Mrs. Gavras feel the same way?"

CG laughed. "Yes - Oui – she would…why do you think we've been married for 25 years. We're partners on every film, partners in life and partners in crime when it comes to SEX. So, don't worry about my wife other than the fact she is a line producer on the film. If you wind up working with her one day, she will not FUCK you even if she knows you're fucking me."

Mona shook her head. "What are you exactly suggesting Mr. Gavras?"

"I've got it. You worked as a diplomat of some type? Am I right or what?"

Mona looked through the man. How the fuck did he nail it?

"And that's what I need. I need a woman to play the attaché of a diplomat at the U.S. Embassy in Santiago, Chile. It's not a large part but a critical one. You have two lines with Jack Lemmon. We'll get your scene shot in two days but bring you down to Mexico City for a week, all expenses paid and cut you a check for $2500. We shoot in 3 weeks. What do you say?"

"Yes, but I'm not saying yes to anything romantic with the director of the film. Are we clear?"

CG smiled into a busted smile and said, "Be careful what you wish for."

Mr. Plaid appreciated her story. Plaid was big on ETHICS and liked the fact that this woman he was sitting across from seemed principled.

Their relationship evolved slowly. But eventually Mr. Plaid proved to be all he had claimed. He was a father who lived alone. He was not flippant about exclusivity and demanded it even more than Mona. His girls were cute. They adored their father.

It took a while before Mona figured it out. She wasn't sure if Mr. Plaid ever saw it.

The signs were there to see…the oldest daughter festered a jealous rage, caged cleverly but nevertheless detectable by a woman like Mona.

There were no issues with the younger girl. She was a party girl. The more bodies, the better and so friendly to all and any nice stranger.

So, any relationship with Plaid would depend on getting over that hurdle. It was that obvious to a woman as intelligent as Mona. The older girl worried. She worried that she would lose her father even more so to an attractive, smart and confident woman.

But Mona had experienced life as a diplomat and with a slow, steady resolve she built a relationship with the older daughter. The fact that younger daughter liked *the woman* didn't hurt either. The girls may have been five years apart, but they were thick-as-thieves and wouldn't have made any kind of a move that decided life for both of them without both of them being in on the decision.

The intimacy came as slow as molasses but when it came, it REALLY CAME.

The fairy tale ending had Mr. Plaid and his Mona living happily ever after, but that's not how it went down.

A commitment was made. A day was set. They would be married at a swanky downtown Chicago hotel where the reception would also take place.

However, Mr. Plaid didn't show.

Mona felt jilted till she spied a TV in the bar at the hotel that blared with a news headline about a dressed in his tux groom-to-be, shot dead in the head. "At this time, the police have no suspects, merely a *person of interest* they want to talk with."

That *person of interest* was the ex-wife who wanted her man back. Mr. Plaid refused to abandon his commitment to Mona, even though it cost him his life. The EX was tried and found guilty and sentenced to life without parole.

Neither Plaid nor his EX - had relatives. They both had been orphans which made them uniquely in common with one another when they met.

It took almost a year with the assistance of a legal eagle to convince DCFS (Department of Children & Family Services) that what Mona wanted, Mona got.

Mona petitioned to be the guardian for the girls and since there was no other family interested in raising them, her wish was granted…a wish that brought bliss and an elusive shade of happiness to the diplomat who won the love of the thick-as-thieves sisters.

What had been tragic, turned into a fairy tale happy ending that no one would have expected.

But It's Just a Plant

We met at the end of mass at St. Mary of Gostyn.

The *Gostyn* referred to a village in Poland. The village in America where I lived was filled with loads of Polish immigrants who had assimilated into the RED, WHITE & BLUE experience in the friendly confines of Downers Grove, a western suburb of Chicago. Downers Grove was a place where you could still keep your doors unlocked so the kids could come and go without having to have a key; kids have a tendency to lose those.

Pastor James often said stuff that mattered little to me but this invitation I couldn't help but act on. "So, if any of you good parishioners would like to take a poinsettia home, feel free since the Christmas season is officially over with the celebration of the Epiphany," (known by many as Three Kings Day). I was surprised that the pastor made such an offer. I thought of him as being a bit of a niggardly man, seeing as how he had failed to keep his commitment to the 501c3 not-for-profit Community Adult Day Care (CADC) where I worked as a volunteer. CADC served adults with cognitive and physical disabilities and by doing so, helped many a caregiver, get some very needed time off to do errands or just chill from the constant needs of their beloved. The parish of Father James had been one of the original twelve churches who came together to form the charity.

They each pledged to contribute at least $1,000 annually and if possible, to recruit volunteers to help keep CADC operating.

Unfortunately, out of the twelve, there was a Judas Iscariot …that being Father James, who refused to meet the stipend. And may I add the only church and pastor to do so and regretfully, my pastor at my parish of 28 years. I saw some great pastors and some not so great and then I saw Father James, which isn't saying much.

I thought, "What the heck? I should take a poinsettia, maybe two. One to bring to CADC and one to make the kitchen a bit festive."

I realized after I took the plants and delivered them to their new owners, one of which was me, that for my own sanity, I had to drop my dislike for the good father. I think I could have handled it sooner if he just said a sweet simple "NO," in his email response to my request that SMG keep their promise to fund the mission of the charity. That email response only came after we spoke on the phone, emailed each other, and then had a meeting that the good father didn't attend. He sent a deacon which meant that the underling would not be able to give us a definitive answer. The question was simple. Would St. Mary of Gostyn (SMG) pay the stipend as all the other churches had done? I was told by the deacon that he was sure Father James would "continue to support CADC." I found those three words with the anagram disingenuous. We were there to find out WHY for the last three years SMG had stopped supporting CADC. The deacon assured me that Father James would con-tact me soon via email.

The email response from the good father was RAW. It wasn't a simple "NO." It was a "NO" filled with denigrating remarks about CADC's Board of Directors who in the good father's viewpoint failed to properly invoice the parish.

I could see the pastor's point, but I didn't hesitate to reply to him quickly with an email that said, "Of the twelve churches, only St. Mary of Gostyn has ever requested an invoice. The other churches don't require one to keep their commitment. I'll be glad to send an invoice if that's all it takes."

That response didn't fare well. I immediately got an email from the good father noting that "St. Mary of Gostyn doesn't have the funds to waste on a charity we know little about." My explicit notation about a "commitment," was a "commitment that came and went a long time ago in his eyes – so, "NO, we have no intention of paying what you call a stipend. We contribute to charities we are familiar with and yours doesn't fall into that category, that's on you, not SMG."

So, I countered. *Well, how about allowing us to have a liaison from the parish to CADC even if you can't give the stipend at this time?*

The "NO" to that was BRUTAL.

So, I couldn't help myself. I had to lay some guilt on the good father because we lived in different worlds. I – yes – I – the layman would pray for the esteemed priest/pastor – *that God would bless him with the gift of EMPATHY for the elderly…a plateau that someday Father James would reach in the near and foreseeable future.* That last ITALIC phrase was a reminder to Father James that what is written in the stars could be a paradise moment of karma that eventually would come back and bite the man, not to be confused with a HOLY MAN - in the ass.

The good father, as they now say in the era of drumpf, doubled-down and attacked me with a plethora of ad hominem arguments that would have made a sailor's face turn to a ghostly snowy shade of pale.

And with that we set the tone for a war between basically two good men. Neither of those dudes, and, yeah, I know I'm talking about ME, should have looked down on their counterpart's perspective. But that's what we did in the land of tribalism.

You bet your sweet ass (black, white, red or yellow – it makes no difference) that I made damn sure the good father knew that I knew that his TAKE was antithetical to the wishes of Christ…wow, that pissed him off. The nerve of a layman to challenge a man of the cloth…the fucking nerve! What was the 21st Century becoming? A land of fools who had the nerve to challenge the protocol that Mother Church knows best. Yeah, for sure! Of course, Mother Church knew best when to keep its trap shut regarding the sad pathetic antics known as predator priests – men preying (and I don't mean the holy type) on boys. Now that truly is DEPLORABLE…thank you Hillary.

Not a PEEP. ALL communication via email fell to a grisly death.

BUT – I - wasn't done. Priest or no Priest, I could give a shit. The motherfuckers needed to get REAL.

There is nothing quite like the *pocket* of the purse. That *pocket* probably is why the Woolworth's lunchroom counter finally integrated during the era of the battle for Civil Rights. When the GREEN went missing from everything ELSE at Woolworth's… that *colored skin could buy…* was when Woolworth wanted to talk. I wasn't sure my ha-ha-lunchroom-counter-protest - would be as effective, but I went ahead and did it anyway. When I now cut a check for the weekly contribution to SMG, I only made it out for one dollar noting in the memo that $19 would be sent to CADC. Which is what I did, figuring that 52 weeks of $19 checks would amount to $988.00…very close to what SMG had pledged. I don't think anyone was going to care about the $12 difference which I could include on the last Sunday check of the year. I could handle another $12 on that final check. That in a nutshell was how I played the *pocket* of the purse game. It was more symbolic than…hmmm…well, you know.

So, that poinsettia I took home meant a lot to me.

And then I noticed it drooping and that made me concerned for a PLANT in the strangest of ways. It was as if the PLANT could communicate with me. I could hear it. "Help me…help me…help me please, I'm fading." I'm not sure why I experienced that spectacular moment, but I did. I couldn't help but say to myself, "Damn it. What can I do to help this PLANT? It deserves to live longer." I wasn't sure how much longer. I just thought – LONGER.

I googled to find out what might be good for a PLANT.

The atmosphere of a hot house was a sure way of perking up my PLANT.

From that moment on, I took that PLANT with me into a steamy shower, placing it a little out of the way of the stream of hot water but close enough to enjoy the humid mist. I thought maybe when I pee in the shower, I should pee a little on my PLANT…so I did, and I think my PLANT liked it based on renewed bud activity. A wee bit of OJ each morning also was something I came up with even if I didn't find it on the all-knowing google. OJ always perked me up. Why not my PLANT?

After exiting the bathroom, I grabbed my PLANT and placed it on the ottoman against the front bay windows for the sunlight it needed after experiencing a bit of Costa Rican humidity via my daily shower. Unfortunately, in Downers Grove during the opening week of January there was no convenient Costa Rican weather, even with climate change. And please, don't tell me you're a doubter when it comes to science. Do what the Indians have always done best. Note the signs. Just note the fucking signs…you know what they are as well as I do, so don't ask me to enumerate them.

If we have but just one WORD to convince you – then let it be WATER.

WATER was placed on a person's forehead to signify purification or regeneration and admission to the Christian Church. Today – a baptism is a baptism of fire - because NOW we have to figure out how to deal with a global crisis when it comes to WATER. When the earth heats up, and no one denies that (on either side of the issue), the waters of the earth get a tad warmer. When water warms - it EXPANDS - and leads to devastating floods, the kind you haven't seen in over 100 years…but WAIT – WAIT – WAIT - you no longer have to WAIT for FATHER TIME to knock off another century…try more like a week or two, a reprise by Mother Nature in this world undergoing climate change to make sure we know who really, is the boss.

I was inspecting my PLANT every day. We were engaged in our morning cup of OJ together and then our morning shower together and then arriving at the ottoman empire together to feel the warm glorious glow of sunlight.

That's where I left my PLANT every day. The next morning we'd start the process all over – sort of like groundhog day.

So, when I took the TIME to THINK about all of this… my immersion into parenthood via a PLANT demanded that I ask myself, "WTF am I doing?"

I knew the answer even though saying it aloud risked me being ridiculed. But when you LOVE another SOUL – another ESSENCE (for those of you who argue that SOUL might be a bit too much) – you fail to realize that BLISS, SERENITY, and HAPPINESS can be enjoyed by another form of life that's not human. It really is all in the giving, so much more than receiving although a *present* a.k.a. in Espanol as *el regalo,* does sound richer to the ears. Or am I taxing you for using a bit of Spanish? After all, if I'm an American, I need to listen to the histrionics of those who often dictate, "Speak English buddy – we don't tolerate that Mexican shit in this country!"

Here's what I will confess to which I pray no one will make fun of. I was thinking of someone who had been in my life, who I lost through the fields of destruction rampant in the opioid 21st Century. My beloved didn't deserve that. No one did. My PLANT reminded me of that shade of pale, that green icky shade of pale on my loved one's face who we lost as the Sun went to hell.

I know I have to die. Don't all living creatures on Mother Earth come to that end?

But damn me to eternal fire if I don't treat my PLANT with LOVE. My PLANT GIVES to me (not the other way around) HOPE - HOPE that someday I'll find that beleaguered soul. He was way too young to be overwhelmed by the evil that took him from us. He didn't deserve to leave earth that way. The least I could do was bid him farewell, but fate didn't allow me to do it on my timeline.

I remember that day like it was yesterday, a nightmare that snuffs out a little bit of me every time I have it. I fear going through that again which I know will never happen except in my mind but too many fools have caused the loss of so much life that one can't help but wonder no matter how you age, "Will I have to face that again?"

My PLANT doesn't attack anyone. That's why I love my PLANT.

My PLANT had me caring for an entity I never considered capable of communicating with. I held in my heart emotions and feelings for that PLANT along with a sense of purpose that Buddha could appreciate; "Love everything; you will be happiest." I could love My PLANT because My PLANT mattered; it was part of life. I had spun a shiny chrysalis that had freed my mind and my spirit to hope for a life filled with bliss. I checked my fetish desires to serve comeuppance to that HOLY MAN – Father James. I found myself taking fresh bread, be it a loaf of wheat, barley, Italian or French that CADC received free of charge each Thursday from Panera and delivered it to my nemesis, the good father. I made sure each loaf was accompanied by a CADC brochure that highlighted what we did for the older folks we served who suffer from dementia and/or physical disabilities. The CADC manna from heaven would be wrapped in a cellophane bag with a red or yellow ribbon depending on my shade of pale that day. And to think, my journey down that road started with a plant that was much, much, more than just a poinsettia.

My PLANT was probably a pacifist, but that was okay with this very fucked up brother-in-arms. Maybe the suffering would have vanished had I taken the trip to the other side, as I contemplated upon hearing of the loss of my beloved. But if I'm honest, I must admit that I was glad to be alive. When I held that thought I noticed my epidermis turn warm as my blood radiated through my skin leaving it with a poinsettia rosy shade of pale.

Yes, Virginia, it's okay to enjoy such bliss even if a FOOL tells you, "It's just a PLANT."

Insomnia

I laid in bed, but I tossed and turned.

Tomorrow would be here soon enough, and I knew I had to get some sleep. I didn't want to disappoint my mother. Somehow my mother had convinced me that her youngest adult son needed *help* and the best way to garner that *help* would be to travel to or maybe more accurately make a pilgrimage to Međjugorje in what was then known as Yugoslavia – a state that no longer exists.

Međjugorje now is in the sovereign state of Croatia. But that had yet to happen and would require a civil war to break up the union of Slavic states that became better known as YUGO (the word "united" in the SLAVIC tongue) unified by one man, the incomparable hero of the Balkans who whipped Hitler's ass and then took on BIG MEAN RED JOE STALIN… letting him know that he, TITO, would bathe Mother Russia's sons in crimson if they even dared to encroach upon the borders of YUGOSLAVIA. Such insolence normally would end up with a BEAR mauling the insolent politician and/or his country. But in this case, STALIN knew he couldn't ask the mothers to give up any more sons after losing so many in the war to end all wars…oops, that was the 1st one and it seems it took a 2nd one to finally bring that home. And besides, TITO, claimed to be a communist, which is what Russia supposedly was, albeit controlled by a politburo of ELITE rich and powerful communists. By declaring himself to be a communist, TITO alleviated Moscow's concern that the dictator of YUGOSLAVIA would align itself with the U.S. Even if it had wanted to do that, the U.S. of A would have been reluctant to form an alliance with anyone calling himself a communist.

From what I ascertained during our travels to the Adriatic Coast, from a priest who couldn't speak a word of English but was fluent in Spanish, a language I wasn't great at but one where I could hold my own, I learned a great deal about TITO. I had studied Spanish in college for two years and then rather quickly I had an opportunity to exercise that knowledge into actual use for my gig with the foreign language radio stations that mainly broadcast in ESPANOL. The good father confided in me, an American, but only after he had checked my passport. I could only imagine that he had secrets he didn't want to share, but who do you trust in a secret police state. And yes, TITO demanded complete and utter loyalty and had an extensive accomplished secret police bureau, but other than that was beloved by those who considered him a hero.

You basically could do whatever you wanted to do in TITO's YUGOSLAVIA. You could work in the field you wanted to work in; the state wouldn't force you to take a job you weren't interested in. You could build a business, a home, work or travel to a different country without interference, like Germany or wherever in Europe. The only thing you couldn't do was criticize TITO.

When you think about it, for a communist regime, that was liberal. So, there were many who liked the stability of TITO's government and his progressive measures to give anyone the economic opportunity to not only say mercy, mercy, please reward my hard work with the riches that come with building a better mouse trap.

TITO was big on defense and he maintained an astute technologically advanced weaponry-systems-military. The SLAVS feared the Russians, but as long as they had Uncle TITO (a truly cherished soul) running things - the Russians could go FUCK themselves. I don't actually believe the good father used the word "chinga" in ESPANOL - consider that a wee bit of license on my part.

So why did I go on that trip with my mother. I guess I knew it was important to her and so I agreed even though I doubt I would have picked that trip. But now in retrospect MOM knew exactly what she was doing. She could see how much I hurt after my fiancé dumped me on the day of our wedding. It was a bit like *THE GRADUATE*, the Mike Nichols film that made Dustin Hoffman a star. The DUDE my fiancé had been having Kama Sutra show-and- tell with — actually - was there to walk her back down the aisle away from the altar and me. However, unlike the film they didn't run to catch a bus as Benjamin Braddock and Elaine did. The DUDE had a Lamborghini Gallardo that ran about 119K at the time, so he was GOLD and I'm sure my fiancé lived happily ever after.

When you get dumped over your earning power, that really sucks and just like they often said on shock radio, can you spell - L-O-S-E-R?

The reception went on. Mother was paying for it and she decided that a party might not be a bad idea. She set the tone by proclaiming that her son had been blessed even if the day appeared to be one filled with loss. "It wasn't meant to be, so let's start the healing now! Let's party and let my son know what you mean to him and what he means to you." There were no vituperative remarks made by Mother about Arlene, the girl who jilted me at the altar and then had a perfect EXIT that made any woman secretly admit if not openly, "Oh, I'd do that as well!" They may very well have been thinking about the physique of DUDE, his royal Caribbean tan and his thick mane of hair that literally screamed mercy, mercy! He was celestial, a man, women would want to get into trouble with.

So, how does a pilgrimage make up for what a young red blooded American male thought was going to be at least a month's worth of intensive passion and love making? But in some ways, it did. I saw things on that trip that were mystifying. Upon my return, I told my siblings that I would not tell them what I saw, because they would doubt it as much as Thomas the Apostle did back in the day.

But I know what I saw and what others standing right next to me couldn't see. It was very much a matter of faith. Faith is something I've never lacked. Maybe it goes back to my brush with death as a three-year-old almost swallowed up by a speeding car that tossed upon impact a three-year-old rag doll tyke into the air to land head first onto or should I say INTO a bumper…a bumper that then had an indentation in it. I saw things at that young age that I never shared until a dozen years later with my parents who simultaneously looked at each other and said, (I swear!) "Did you tell him that?" That's when I knew I had dazzled them regarding my floating above that operating table that wasn't some hallucinatory fluke. Mercy, mercy, PLEASE, I was in outer space with the feeling of the SUN toasting me with a warmth I've never felt before. It was frankly orgasmic and for many men they have no idea of what I'm talking about. Unfortunately, men have ejaculation confused with a Kama-Sutra show-and-tell orgasm and that just isn't even worthy of a mercy, mercy, PLEASE!

Our trip to YUGO defied the laws of science. Mom and I made that trip up the side of that mountain to the large white blazing cross that had at times beamed flashes of light – almost like lightning. Fortunately, they had made paths to handle the traffic. There were strange sightings that were scientifically in the SUN and its universe that would be hard to describe without the word "miraculous" mentioned.

Mom carried a rosary with her…the same one she had had for over forty years having gotten it on her wedding day with my father. Yes, they were both religious, my mother maybe a bit more so than my dad, but he had his moments.

When Father was told that he had best get all of his wife's affairs in order and make plans to raise three kids by himself in maybe six or seven months, he got down on his knees and pleaded mercy, mercy, PLEASE!

His prayers were answered. Mother got an experimental medication that could supposedly cure TB – tuberculosis - also known as consumption. She wasn't supposed to get the actual medication. She was supposed to get the control sugar pill that had no effect, but Providence played a part in pulling them closer. A nurse that had been a colleague of Mother's in another hospital where they both worked as R.N.'s made sure that her former nurse buddy got the good stuff.

Mother was healed.

I was deathly afraid that Mother would fall down on that trip as we went up and down the mountain to see that white blazing cross. Both her ankles and mine were swollen that evening before we climbed into our respective beds in a bunk bed that we had to share when we stayed at the farmer's house, just outside of Medjugorje, where all the wonders occurred. The next day, neither of us complained of any pain and our ankles somehow deflated to normal. That just shouldn't have happened. We didn't have any Ibuprofen to bring the swelling down but down it was when we awoke.

The farmer and his family couldn't have been sweeter. Fortunately, their oldest daughter, a high school senior knew how to speak Spanish. She and I, would work everything out, even what we watched on TV. Some of the movies were American and so that was a no-brainer. Yeah, it was subtitled in SLAV, but Mother and I could certainly hear the English in the background, but who watches TV on a trip like that?

Mother's rosary turned. The links between the beads before we arrived were all silver. By the time we left, the links had gone through a Chrysalis…half of the link was silver, the other half was GOLD as GOLD as DUDE.

Just like they say it in the SUN, I could actually look at that globe that shined so bright and find on half of that star a HOST with the letters IHS (a monogram for the Christ embossed on the white satin bread) and a CHALICE filling up the other 50% of that bright ball of light.

That trip did wonders for my psyche. My Mother and I became even closer. I loved and adored that woman. She was my SUN.

I'm not sure when I would have considered dating again, yet alone Kama Sutra show-and-tell, but I must say, that trip did wonders for my aura. I can happily report that I now enjoy a rosy shade of pale that still wants to get into trouble.

When I find the right one, I'm sure that I'll be verklempt over the anticipation that I am going to get in trouble again with someone I want. Oh, I have to have that!

I looked for love in someone's eyes because I loved being in trouble, but this time LORD - could I find peace without the need of anyone? Until that dawn when I meet my intergalactic partner who won't stand me up at an altar, I'll be content with the peace and BLISS that comes with being happy in being who I am. Then and only then will I be free from my insomnia of woe and worry that I may never fall in love again.

Mercy, mercy, PLEASE LORD! When I asked Mr. M.D. of what was ailing me, he said, "All you really need is Good Lovin' – Lovin' in the morning, Lovin' in the afternoon, Lovin' in the evening with a baby squeezing you tight. If you can find that, your shade of pale will be just FINE – and - you'll no longer have the fever but the CURE." Thank you, my fine Young Rascals.

Music makes me happy, blissful for sure, but no doubt, you've probably noticed.

That Late Night Call

It was 1:30 in the morning. I was UP. I just couldn't shut out of my brain what had happened to my beloved who passed in the beat of a moment in a time zone that was way – way - too young. I was on my couch with my trusty dog, SYD, by my side while I banged on the keyboard of my APPLE creating the next great American novel when my cell lit up. I usually kill the ring tone late at night which is the only time when I bang the keyboard, be it my beloved Baby Grand or my APPLE. My first thought was, *I don't recognize that number…I ain't picking it up. Shit? Who calls at 1:30 in the morning? I'm pickin' it up!*

"Hello?"

"Hello…I'm uh….

I was intrigued. It was a silky feminine voice.

"I'm uh…not doing-to-good. I'm contemplating suicide."

"Whoa!" I replied. "By all means, let's talk."

There was a good deal of silence on the line. I considered broaching it, but then thought better. I didn't need to talk. I needed to be a LISTENER.

"I'm uh….am a…a mother of a six-year-old. I have a husband who doesn't work…well, that's sounds a bit harsh, but it's true. He will get a job and keep it for no more than three weeks – tops!"

"And does your husband know how you feel?"

"Of course, he does. That's why it's so frustrating!"

There was a bit of silence on the line to either give me the chance to grasp what a woman just said to me in complete candor of the heart or it was on me to keep the repartee going, but to do neither wasn't an option.

"Actually, my husband and I are separated and have been for almost a year. I don't want to go back with him."

"So, what's with the talk of suicide?" There, I said it.

"It's just too much. I have to keep it all together for our six-year-old. And, well… I'm lonely."

"Aren't we all?"

"Are you telling me that a sensitive guy like you, willing to talk at this hour to a perfect stranger is lonely?" The spoken word can shock in a way that's not apparent in type – especially when it's shocking to hear it broken down into parts….LONE-EH-LY.

"Yeah, I too am lonely. I was set to get married. I was so in love with the woman. At the altar - YES – the altar is where she dumped me in front of family and friends. Just picture the film, *THE GRADUATE*, in your head when Benjamin Braddock grabs the winsome bride to be and off-they-go. Now place me in the spot where the groom was standing and you've captured the cinematic moment of my life, which I certainly can't describe to you any better than what rolled up on that Mike Nichols film."

"Well, that puts a whole new twist on this phone call." I could hear her breath recaptured.

"I like the sound of that."

Quiet. Silence brewed on that cellular wave when I heard the mystique of my caller's voice. It was very feminine. "Well, then I think I'm putting a hold on my date with destiny."

"Wow! That's great!"

"And you know why?"

I didn't so I kept it real. "NO…uh, I don't."

"YOU, silly!"

"Me?"

"Yeah, you LISTENED, really LISTENED. Where did you get your training as a suicide hotline operator?"

"A what?" Now I was confused.

"You're not a suicide hotline counselor?" The word "counselor" had a *cunt* like sound to it when she weighed in heavy on the *coun* of counselor."

"No, why'd you think that?" I was intrigued at "Hello," but this twist was simply the best.

"You helped me to take my heart and make it strong. So, what part of Saskatchewan are you in?"

"I'm not. What area code did you try to call?"

"639?"

"Ah, that's Saskatchewan." I had been doing business with a company in that area code. So as soon as she said "639," I knew where she was. "You must have inadvertently dialed 630…I'm just outside of Chicago, Illinois in the States."

"You're not with SUICIDE HOTLINE?"

"No, I'm not a counselor. I was up trying to bang out the great American novel."

"You're simply the best. You took my call in the wee hours of the morning to let me tear up your phone. I suppose I'm sleeping in Saskatchewan, but somehow I'd love to meet you."

I didn't know how to answer that, so I let her continue. "Yes, we must meet even if it's just to give me an opportunity to thank you. I hoped beyond hope that you were down the street and we could somehow have coffee."

"I like coffee. Let's do it."

It's been 25 years since we met through the galaxy of fate. A wrong number *sometimes* is a right number. It was for me…

it was for us. I made the trek to Saskatchewan and I found someone who helped me overcome my LONELY heart. I became a Canadian and reveled at saying the word "about," in the flavor of a Maple Leaf – pronouncing it as A – BOOT. It made my States-side friends chuckle to hear me turning into Dudley Do-Right or was it - Sergeant Preston of the YUKON?

But I was happy with a woman that was simply the best… better than all the rest…better than anyone I'd ever met. Please enjoy my homage to Ms. Tina Turner performing that classic written by Holly Knight and Mike Chapman.

The life I saved that night was the life that saved me. I'm not sure how it came about.

The dad who had little contact if any with the six-year-old allowed me to adopt the child. She became mine as much as her mother's. That little girl with a pumpkin shade of pale that was just so darn cute stole my heart.

Sometimes when our hearts are on fire and we lose everything in our world of dreams, we actually wind up with a stronger heart. A stronger heart that knows how to deal with adversity, a heart that won't bust when life turns to shit, which always happens to everyone.

I view what I once saw as tragic now as a blessing. Yes, it was humbling to be left standing at the altar with my dick in my hand. BUT - God had blessed me with a partner that is simply the best, better than all the rest and my one & only which can't be topped ever.

'And to think it all came about by that late-night call that should have been dismissed as "You've got the wrong number, Miss."

I'm grateful that my inner self told me to pick up that call and to keep listening and when a word of encouragement was needed, to give it freely without conditions.

If that isn't BLISS for two lonely souls, I don't know what is?

That Damn TV Set

Every weekday morning the alarm was set to go off precisely at 6:30 a.m. It provided me a two and a half hour window to take a shower, get dressed in a suit, tie and dress shirt picked out the night before, grab some coffee, slightly toast a Bays English Muffin with a bit of melted butter and cinnamon on it and then catch the express Metra Train for the 23 minute commute to NBC in downtown Chicago. A young father with two kids and a randy wife had to have every drop of that sleep potion before that screaming shock-jock clicked on a radio set on the nightstand next to our bed. As to any other distraction, God help any neighbor who made a ruckus at that early hour that might wake me from my slumber.

So, what was the deal? It was only 6 a.m. and how the hell did the TV in the front room visible from the master bedroom magically turn on? I nudged my wife Arletta, but she flipped onto her other side. She didn't care if the TV came on; she could sleep through anything and 6:30 a.m. was a long 30 minutes away on this Monday, the start of the week.

When we did arise each morning, the routine was set in stone. I suppose it will sound selfish, but I didn't find it that way since most of the men I knew expected the same – getting themselves ready to head off to work while the little woman took care of the kids. It still was a time when the man was the main bread-winner and the wife was a homemaker taking care of the needs of their young. And so, Arletta tended to the two girls, one at 7 ½ and the other one at only 2 1/2. Both girls had different needs. The older one, Renee, had to have her breakfast, wash her face and hands, get dressed into her St. Priscilla uniform, gather her book bag and walk to school with her friend and classmate Ashley accompanied by Ash's mother, who Arletta counted as a friend. The baby had to be fed and demanded attention. Gina wanted to play.

As a young executive I had to make myself look professional for my position as the Marketing & Promotion Director for WMAQ, the Channel 5 owned and operated NBC television station located at the Merchandise Mart. It was the mid-80's and television stations competed with Chicago's major newspapers including the Tribune and the Sun-Times, for the minds and hearts of Chicagoans. Competition for customer allegiance was fierce which increased the value and importance of a solid promotion director.

The only station that wasn't considered a "competitor" may have been the most welcome. WTTW – Channel 11, the PBS station was beloved by all even by the GM's at the commercial stations. WTTW wasn't a threat to anyone. Their ratings were minimal compared with the network operations and they served a purpose that the commercial venues were no longer interested in. They provided children's programming and documentaries; a loss leader that TV execs might publicly applaud but privately spurned.

When I finally climbed out of that bed to turn off the TV, I was surprised to find my daughter Renee siting Indian style in front of the set mesmerized by some guy singing in a somewhat nasal voice albeit on key - the words, "Won't you be my neighbor?" I took a deep breath and within a moment of seeing how engaged she was with the guy on the screen I lost my annoyance because it was my Pumpkin, the apple of my eye. I loved the baby, but there's nothing quite like your first born... they steal a part of your heart that is only meant for them.

"Renee, why are you up so early honey?"

Renee put her finger to her mouth. "Shhh daddy...pleassse...I'm watching Mister Rogers."

Without saying a word out loud I asked myself, "Who the hell is Mr. Rogers?" So, I watched the show with her and hated it but kept that to myself. After that initial disturbance, I never tried to stop Renee from turning the set on at 6 a.m. If Pumpkin loved Mr. Rogers – that was good enough for me.

Through a strange turn of events and the search firm Heidrick & Struggles, I found myself a short while later leaving NBC and accepting an offer to work for WTTW as their new Corporate Communications Chief. In my new position, I oversaw internal employee communications and communiques addressed to the board of directors, publicity & promotion for both the local and national programming produced by Window To The World, Inc. and publication of ELEVEN Magazine, the monthly periodical that was sent to the 160,000 subscribers of WTTW.

SUCCESS BREEDS THAT WHICH YOU
SOMETIMES DON'T WANT

The very first challenge at WTTW, besides building a communications department, which meant hiring the best people, was the promotion and publicity for the play, *Huckleberry Finn* that featured a local Chicago actor, Meshach Taylor on his way up. Meshach won an Emmy for his solid performance in the WTTW production before he headed off to Broadway and then onto the hit TV series, *Designing Women.* I got a chance to talk a good deal with Taylor who was willing to do whatever to promote the upcoming televised drama.

Those in the business marveled at the blinding spotlight of publicity and press generated for Meshach, for WTTW and for the teleplay *Huckleberry Finn.* Daily papers had TV listing guides that came with their Sunday edition and somehow, I secured 5 covers featuring Meshach. This was a feat that had never been accomplished for any Channel 11 production. The word spread that the promotion guru WTTW just hired was so good that it would be just a matter of time before PBS out of Alexandria, Virginia would try to recruit him for the network.

Technically PBS wasn't a network, it was an association or a system of stations that came together and pooled their programming for national consumption, but the general public never knew that distinction. Nevertheless, I was hot!

By the time the next big challenge had to be met, I had hired a number of seasoned publicists, editorial and promotion personnel that could deal with the complex issues of launching a national program. They were also adept at our attempt to secure publicity for WTTW's upcoming 30th anniversary which included a visit by Fred Rogers to Chicago.

So, when I got a call from David Newell, the publicist for the show who also played the character known as Mr. McFeely, the deliveryman, a.k.a. affectionately as Mr. Speedy Delivery, I was a bit surprised that a national show needed someone to pull double duty - but that was how it sometimes rolled in public television. On the upside, I loved the fact that we, David and me, could talk turkey about promoting and publicizing a show and a show talent. Fred Rogers would do whatever WTTW desired regarding the publicity of the station's 30th Anniversary. We both understood that for each correspondent, each reporter, each radio or TV host, we had to give them an angle that made their coverage unique.

"Would you be so kind to send me a fax of the proposed schedule of Fred meeting with the media in Chicago and a bit of a bio regarding each interviewer?"

The fax went out 4 days later.

David Newell called.

"Fred genuinely loved the schedule of press you booked for his appearance in Chicago but was disappointed with one detail." He paused to give me a chance to ask a question, but I waited. "May I respectfully ask, how come you don't have Fred on Oprah. Oprah tapes in Chicago. He wants to be on Oprah."

"David, I'm not sure he's a guest that Oprah would necessarily want. Oprah's not comfortable around kids."

"How do you know that?"

"I know her executive producer Debra - Debbie Dee and trust me, Oprah's not going to welcome Fred to the show."

"Well, do we need to discuss this with Mr. McCarter?"

I knew when I was getting jammed and there was no point in engaging with somebody who wanted blood and who had prominence on a national television program. Talent always wins those battles.

"Let me see what I can do David. In the meantime, I'll fax you in detail all of the appointments, all the locations where Fred needs to be and a bit of background on whoever he is meeting with."

"Wait, I detect something by that statement that's troubling. May I ask… uh, you're going to be with us during the three days?" David's question had caught me off guard. I now had a department with 24 employees to run and I had already made up my mind to assign Nancy Volino, one of my best publicists to spend the 72 hours with Fred and Dave when they arrived in Chicago. My days of going around with a client were over as far as I was concerned.

"David, you'll have one of my best publicists working with you. Her name is Nancy Volino. She came to us from CBS, so you and Fred are in good hands."

"No, no, no! Your reputation precedes you. We want you. Do I have to ask Mr. McCarter about this?"

This was becoming a very uncomfortable phone call. "David, I've got to get to a meeting. As I said, I'll get you an updated fax, a complete agenda of all that we've already booked for newspapers, radio and TV interviews with Fred. We can discuss this Oprah request later since we fortunately have a bit of time... but I think you'll like Nancy."

"Okay. Go to your meeting but Fred wants you."

WHAT FRED WANTED – FRED GOT

After a visit to the corner office and a succinct but direct conversation with WTTW's CEO, Mr. McCarter, I was reminded that the publicity campaign for Fred Rogers' arrival in Chicago would have great impact on the bottom line of WTTW's pledge drive, occurring at the same time. I was told in no uncertain terms spoken in blood that I had to somehow get Rogers on Oprah's show and be the ONE who would shepherd Mr. Rogers while he was in the Windy City.

Once that line of demarcation was established, I made a call to an associate producer that I knew at ABC7 where Oprah's show was taped. In spite of my conviction that Fred Rogers would never be welcomed on the show, I had to at least try and ask.

"Hi Sally. Hey, I've got Fred Rogers coming into town; would you consider booking him on the show? After a slight pause, she said, "Hmmm, let me bring that up with the team and I'll get back to you." I was shocked. I expected a rejection with maybe a reason or maybe a sign I could share with David and Fred so that we could finally put that request to R.I.P. I was certain that the Oprah Winfrey Show wouldn't even consider having a host from a kids' TV program as a guest since her format tackled issues. Sure, they had celebrities but usually it was a celebrated film star that also had a cause to champion… at least that was my impression. Before we concluded the call, Sally asked a question I didn't expect. "On occasion we do short segments and then package them into an hour – they're usually about 15 minutes, would that be okay?" THAT would be more than acceptable. I'd get Rogers the exposure he coveted without having him deal with a full hour with an Oprah, whom I had heard wasn't kid friendly. "Of course, Sally…yeah, that'd work just fine." I ended the call, hopeful that she'd get back to me in a day or two with a reason, a sign, a line that I could use to free me of the albatross around my neck.

I double checked my list. I even got Santa to check it twice.

It was a mighty line-up that any public relations department would be proud to present as a plan of action for promoting a beloved figure and his merry band of characters that included King Friday XIII, Daniel Striped Tiger, X the Owl, Henrietta Pussycat, Cornflake S. Pecially, Edgar Cooke, Grand-père, and Lady Elaine Fairchilde. I had taken the time to study the show and learn about it from an expert who faithfully woke me up each and every morning at 6 a.m. for our rendezvous in front of that damn TV.

"No Daddy, that's not right. Queen Sara - King Friday's wife doesn't run the Museum Go Around – that's Lady Elaine's job. She's way too cranky, don't you think?"

I still hated the show but at least I was beginning to understand why my daughter found it fascinating. It was a land of make-believe and Fred's presence was engaging, peaceful, comforting and without fanfare…maybe that's why Renee liked the guy so much. He looked right into the lens as if he was talking directly to my daughter and the other kids who watched his show daily. I found him effeminate and maybe that's why as an Italian stallion, I was a bit turned off by him or was it threatened? However, I discovered early in my career from various program execs that how you personally felt about a program or a personality mattered little when it came to how the public felt about their TV favorites.

I couldn't imagine myself spending a Friday, Saturday and Sunday with Fred Rogers and so I did my best to continue to try and convince David that Nancy was perfect for the Chicago junket. But after another summons to the corner office, I resigned myself to being the chosen ONE to chaperone the Pittsburgh guests through a myriad of interviews with various newspaper columnists and the popular TV critics of the day such as Dan Ruth, Rick Kogan, Anna Marie Kukec, Michael Miner, and Gary Deeb not to mention the extremely successful and popular WGN Radio's Roy Leonard who covered TV for the World's Greatest Newspaper's 50,000 watt AM powerhouse.

Having the TV beat at a newspaper, radio or TV venue was a big deal in the mid-80's. The ABC7 television owned and operated network station had literally stolen from the Sun-Times, a guy who had been lured from the Tribune, an acerbic TV critic by the name of Gary Deeb for a rumored 7 figures. The dog-eat-dog environment of TV entertainment and newscast TV rating wars made for good copy and helped to sell papers and in the case of ABC7, attract audience eyeballs that impacted the bottom line of that critical metric – CPM or in layman's terms - media costs per thousands.

The only one who was ecstatic about me spending all of that time with Mister Rogers was Renee.

"Daddy, make sure you get a picture of Mr. Rogers – autographed – okay?"

"Sure, Pumpkin. And what do you want him to write when he signs the pic?"

"To Renee Christine, my number one fan…Mister Rogers." She had a lilt to the phrase – going down in vocal squeakiness on the man's name.

"Really? The only time anyone calls out your middle name tied to your first name is when you're in trouble."

She giggled. "That's okay. There are a lot of Renee's in the world and I don't want anyone in my class to see that autographed picture and not get that it was signed just for me."

I had to nod at the perspicacity of my Pumpkin's observation. She was more than just cute – she was also brilliant.

I was beginning to get the jitters about the assignment. My team had booked every kind of coverage with every kind of angle for a story that you could imagine. We had to. Everybody seemed eager to do a piece on Fred but being a sharp columnist, reporter or journalist demanded a unique concept – not just the same thing everyone else was going to do or the BOSS would come looking for that talent with blood in their eyes. To be successful, we offered the chance to do a back stage look at the rehearsals for his stage shows, his trip to the WTTW studios that included being interviewed by the incomparable John Callaway considered by those in the media biz to be the country's best TV interviewer, his walk on the Michigan Mile as well as his status as the featured guest of honor for a 650 seat dinner held at the Hyatt Regency on that Friday, officially for the press, his first night in the city.

I could guarantee that over the three days numerous radio and TV stations planned to run packages with in-depth reporting about Fred and his commitment to quality programming for children. On his final day, that Sunday, WGN-TV's Robert Jordan planned on doing a LIVE report from the Auditorium between the first and second stage shows. You'd have to be living under a rock in Chicago at that moment to not know that Fred and his trusted Sancho Panza - Mr. McFeely - had arrived in the Second City to celebrate WTTW's 30th anniversary.

The only element missing in the jig saw puzzle was whether Fred was *to-be-or-not-to-be*, with the Queen Bee of Chicago TV talk. In her first year on the air at WLS, she beat Phil Donahue in the 9 to 10 a.m. time slot. That was amazing!

So, what was the hold-up? Why hadn't I gotten a call back from Sally? What a mess! I did what even I knew as a pro to be a sign of desperation. I called Sally back, not once, not twice but three times leaving messages. At this point, I didn't care if the answer was "NO!" We had so much coverage booked that in my mind it didn't really matter – or so I had told myself.

But it did matter. When I called David Newell to update him that Sally had called from the Oprah Show to say, "Thanks but no thanks, buddy– we're taking a pass on Fred," the silence on the line was as dismissive as a bloody eyeball-to eyeball encounter with Dr. Hyde. I waited patiently. The pregnant pause lasted a good 15 seconds before I heard the words, "Oh my, my, my…that just won't do. Do we need to call Mr. McCarter?" Frankly at this point, knowing what we had lined up, I didn't give a rat's ass if Mr. McFeely called BIG BILLY MAC or not.

However, I played it cool and professional. "You know, I've yet to call the Executive Producer of the show. I may not have mentioned that. Her name is Debbie Dee and I could call her directly, although I'm sure – Mr. Speedy Delivery cut me off. "Yeah, why don't you do that sir? Give me a call then. I've got to run."

I started to laugh but the best I could generate was a chuckle. Oh hell, I had nothing to lose, so why not? I checked my Rolodex and there it was – the card with Debbie's direct dial number. For those too young to appreciate what a Rolodex is or was – it's merely - from an engineering standpoint, a collection of cards that literally are attached to a core that rotates. From a professional PR standpoint - it was your bible – how connected by blood or hook or by crook were you? For a guy in his early thirties, I had a 'bitchin' Rolodex filled with the private home and office phone numbers of iconic figures from all walks of life.

Caller ID wasn't on the horizon yet either – so all good for me…surprise, surprise, Debbie picked up her private phone. She was laughing at something and then it was good old Debbie. "Hello, this is Debra, who's calling?"

"Hi Debbie."

"Jeezes! Why are you bothering me about this? You know I nixed the guy and I love him but he's not Oprah material. We focus on topics like feuding families, how fat affects a marriage and that kind of faire. Sure, we'll do a celebrity coming through town now and then but they're usually major film or entertainment TV stars…or maybe you haven't caught the show enough to know that Oprah wouldn't know what to do with a host from a kid's show, so puh-leeze – let it go."

"Yeah, but I need a favor – a big one. You know I left NBC to take this gig-

"Congrats on that! But it's irrelevant."

"Sure, but just give me thirty seconds." There was a pause – so I figured she had started her stopwatch and I had best get my elevator spiel in. "Remember how you needed that footage of that press conference with your G.M. Joe Ahern and the Mayor and the only crew that covered that was our techs for our show, *Chicago Tonight*?"

"What about it?"

"Well I could have told you we didn't have the time to retrieve that – but I didn't. I got our video librarian, James Matsumoto to find that gem for you and we had it ready for pick-up within two hours of your request. Remember how badly you told me you needed that."

"What the fuck, you're going to play that card? Fuck you buddy…that's bullshit. That video was for a local celebration - a sales party – not even a televised event at that and you expect me to put your guy on a show that currently is the number one talk show in Chicago - you consider that parity? Forget it." A slam with that tingle of bell ring made it very final, an experience that Millennials and Generation Z pups probably can't relate to. Deb's rejection of Fred didn't bother me but her calling me out did because I knew I had stepped over the line of press etiquette and now I had a rotten taste in my mouth for the guys from Pittsburgh for their incessant nagging about a booking I knew was nothing short of turning water into wine.

In 1984, ABC7 had brought Oprah to Chicago from Baltimore to serve as a replacement for Robb Weller, eager to get out of his contract as host on a low-rated show called A.M. Chicago. Robb would go on to become TV aristocracy as host of a highly syndicated daily show known as Entertainment Tonight, seen on hundreds of TV stations throughout the U.S. Depending on whom you believe, Oprah had been discovered by either a WLS program exec by the name of Jeff McGrath or the G.M. of

WLS-ABC7, Dennis Swanson. An exec that I worked with at Channel 11, Elizabeth Richter, a former ABC7 employee, who now oversaw the Production Department for both local and national WTTW productions claimed credit as well citing her integral involvement in the discovery of Winfrey.

I suppose the truth of how Oprah wound up in Chicago might be part and parcel to all the claims made because based on my experiences, TV was that kind of medium – one that required collaboration.

In 1985, *A.M. Chicago* dissolved to resurrect into an hour show from the half-hour it had been with the new title: *The Oprah Winfrey Show.* That same year the cinematic director Steven Spielberg signed Winfrey for the part of Sofia for his film, *The Color Purple.* Supposedly the story for public consumption was that Spielberg was in Chicago and had caught Oprah's show in his hotel room and immediately thought, "I've got the woman to play Sofia." However, according to other sources, Oprah had been campaigning for the part of Sofia and had even turned up for an audition for "Moon Song," the secretive working title of Spielberg's adaptation of Alice Walker's book. As the rendition of that tale goes, Oprah waited a good 60 days or so before she called back the casting agency only to receive the dismissive, "Don't call us, we'll call you," mantra that is so integral to the land of the Hollywood blockbuster. Oprah learned from the bitchy casting woman that they were leaning towards Alfre Woodard, "a real actress." The implied put down deflated Oprah who wanted that part so bad that according to Winfrey herself, she literally prayed to get it. However, the casting belittling put her in a tail-spin and for some reason Oprah decided to go to a "fat farm," in the hopes of getting her weight in check and allowing herself time to let the dream slip away when she got a call from Spielberg who expressed his interest in her doing the role but only if she didn't lose a pound.

So, Oprah's star was shining bright in 1985 even though the show had yet to go into syndication which would take place the following year with a deal with KINGWORLD. It was Roger Ebert, the renowned film critic, co-host of the PBS show SNEAK PREVIEWS and for a brief moment - a paramour if only a 'dating' one - who encouraged Oprah to ask ABC for ownership of the show as she competed against the KING of TALK – Phil Donahue in all of America's markets. Jeff Jacobs a high priced and very competent attorney especially at the art of negotiation helped Winfrey win her freedom from WLS to launch a show for national distribution that she would outright own. The debut of the syndicated show was seen in 138 markets with a TV reach of 92% of American households. Jacobs would go on to become the first president and CEO of HARPO Entertainment Group. That "deal" was an incredible feat at that time for television because even Phil's show was owned by a parent company, named Multimedia Entertainment. However, for the purpose of my story, I'm sharing a moment in time in the spring of 1985 when Oprah was still an employee of ABC7 and technically like any other employee, she reported to the new General Manager (G.M.) Joe Ahern and the new Program Director (P.D.), Tim Bennett.

Now the detail, regarding Oprah's new bosses, is critical to the telling of this tale. Yes, Oprah would go on to win the battle against Phil, go on to own her show outright, go on to purchase the old Fred Niles Studios on Chicago's near west side and create her HARPO Studios empire (HARPO is OPRAH backwards) and go on to become a billionaire and some might even say a kingmaker who blessed the Obama candidacy with her fame, wealth and fan base influence to do the unthinkable

– help a black man with a name as funny as hers - move into the White House. But the moment I'm sharing is prior to that meteoric rise in Winfrey's stature.

The new G.M. Joe Ahern and the new P.D. Tim Bennett were people I knew professionally. In Tim's case we enjoyed a friendship; he offered me the opportunity to become his top lieutenant when he ran the marketing and advertising department at ABC7 prior to his ascendency to P.D. The only reason I turned Tim down was that NBC offered me that very same week a position of parity to that of Tim's. It didn't make sense to take an assistant's job when I could be like Tim – a boss of a department. Tim understood and we continued to share a collegial friendship even though we were competitors.

So, when Debbie slammed her phone down to indicate "NO," I should have celebrated knowing that I could honestly tell Fred and Mr. McFeely that the discussion was over - but instead I decided to see if I could go around her. That was professionally a NO-NO, but I had a mission. But before I called one of Oprah's bosses, I thought it best to find out a bit more about Fred Rogers.

I had Lori get from Lenore, the WTTW librarian, copies of numerous articles and tidbits about Fred Rogers. I learned that Fred had worked for the NBC network in New York on musical programs including *Your Hit Parade, The Kate Smith Hour* and *The Voice of Firestone*. He was one of a handful of original employees that WQED, Pittsburgh – the public TV station hired even before it went on the air. He left his behind the scenes work as a puppeteer at WQED to host a children's show for the Canadian Broadcasting Corporation (CBC) and debut as an on-camera personality for a 15-minute children's program entitled *Misterogers*. Like Oprah, Fred acquired the rights to his program from the CBC and moved the show to WQED and the rest was as they say *history*.

Information is power and my impression of Fred as a TV impresario began to change my feelings about him. I still didn't want to be stuck with him for 3 days, but now I had a sense that this guy was a lot smarter than I had given him credit when it came to the business of broadcasting. My next move would be to call Tim Bennett, the P.D. a.k.a. as the Program Director at WLS and try and make an appeal that Rogers was worth having as a guest to talk about not only a kid's show but the status of TV and how the venue was undergoing monumental changes. I was going to do the whole nine yards about Fred's place in American television but as it turned out I didn't have to.

What I found out on that call was Bennet's intense HATRED…maybe that's a bit too strong - so let me amend it to intense DISLIKE of Debbie Dee.

I had known Tim for years. We had been active in the Broadcast Promotion & Marketing Executives (BPME) professional association both appearing on seminars at the national conferences and as board members. In all those years I had never heard Tim utter an expletive – never. The guy was the consummate diplomat and was very selective about his use of language even when talking about competitors. Following my disclosure of my call with Debbie, I was shocked to hear him say the words, "Well, FUCK Debbie. As the P.D. of WLS-TV, I have the authority to book Rogers."

"Wow, that would be awesome Tim."

"Now can it be live to tape? I ask that because I'd actually like to schedule his appearance for a day when the kids are home from school – say Veterans Day."

Veterans Day was several months away but I didn't give a shit. "Sure, no problem. He's in town in two weeks over a Friday, Saturday, Sunday." I provided the specific dates for his Chicago junket and noted that the time of the stage shows on Saturday and Sunday would probably negate an appearance at ABC7 on one of those days unless very early in the day.

"No problem…no stage shows on Friday so - Friday it is. We'll have to hold the crew – they do the show live from 9 to 10 in the morning, then go to lunch…but there's no reason why we can't tape the show during the second portion of the shift. Ok, let's plan on having him here at 11:00 a.m. – we'll roll at 11:30 or so and that way I can release the crew at their normal out without incurring overtime. Sound good?"

"Yeah that's awesome. I'll be with him and I'm probably going to bring a professional still photographer along."

"That's fine but you can't bring a video crew in. I'll have union issues with that."

"You got it – thanks Tim."

"My pleasure – my kids love the guy. Take care."

I put my hands up in the air and said, "YES, THANK YOU LORD!" Lori, my secretary, who sat at a desk just outside my door heard my cry of elation and popped her pringle head in to ask, "Good news?" I smiled back at her and said, "The best! By the way, can you type up a quick memo to the old man stating simply that Corporate Communications has booked Fred Rogers for an appearance on The Oprah Winfrey Show?" Lori smiled and said, "The old man – so – that's what we call Mr. McCarter these days." I smiled back, "Ha-ha – cut the memo and I'll sign it so you can walk it over to Renee (McCarter's executive assistant) and ask her to please give it to the old man A-S-A-P."

The phone rang and Lori gave me a wink to let me know she'd pick it up and screen it. She was a great gatekeeper.

"Hello. WTTW Corporate Communications, may I help you?" Lori listened and nodded. "Let me see if I can track my boss down." She put the call on hold and asked, "Do you want me to ditch her?"

I shook my head. "Nah, I'd better take this."

I picked up the phone and nonchalantly asked, "Debbie, what can I do for you?"

"You can go fuck yourself buddy. I can't believe you went around me – you son-of-a-bitch!"

"Ah –

She cut me off with blood in her voice. "Here's how we're going to play it. You are going to get your own audience. We're not going to find a bunch of rug-rats to fill the seats – and you'll need at least 75 of them – so – that's on you. Oh, and we're not mailing tickets out – I'll send 75 over to you and that's also on you."

"Okay Debbie, that's no big deal. Donna Davies who is coordinating Fred's stage shows won't have a problem busing in a bunch of kids. Donna also secures audiences for our shows, so this will be covered. Anything else?"

"Oprah doesn't want to do this show which leads me to ask, is your guy good at monologues?" She took a pause and I wasn't going to walk into it, so I waited.

"You're going to pay for this, buddy!"

"Is that a threat?"

"No! More like a promise. Have your guy here on time at 11 a.m. sharp." The phone went bang. She had hung up on me twice and we hadn't hit Noon yet.

Lori walked in with the memo. "You approve?"

It was perfectly crafted, and I was about to sign it when the phone rang again. Lori grabbed it and did the usual salutation before she put the call on hold and asked, "Do you want to talk to some guy named Joe Ahern?"

"Holy shit. Ahern's calling?"

Lori nodded.

"Damn, that can't be good." I put my hand through my hair tempted to pull out several follicles.

"Do you want me to stall?"

"Nah, I've got to talk to him. But this memo, Lori, doesn't travel – put it on hold till I know what he wants." Lori stepped out as I took the call. I was concerned that Debbie had gotten to Joe who as the G.M. had the power to overrule the P.D. - Tim Bennett's decision with a checkmate move going to Debbie.

"Hi Joe. What can I do for you?"

"I understand you booked Mister Rogers for an Oprah Show through Tim Bennett." Joe waited for me to confirm.

"Yes. I've known Tim for years. Is there a problem?" I expected that Fred's booking was toast.

"Well I hope not. Are you going to have a professional still photographer with you to cover Rogers' appearance?"

"Joe, I haven't booked anyone yet, but, sure. Why?"

He didn't bother to answer my question but instead asked another. "And you're going to handle the audience and dissemination of the tickets?"

"Yes sir. We've got an experienced audience development office that handles details like that for the shows we tape here."

"So, you'll make sure to save two tickets for my kids? My wife will be with them, but she doesn't want to sit in the audience. She'll stand in the wings but when the show's done, she wants a photo taken of Mister Rogers with her and the kids – okay?"

"Sure, no problem Joe. I'll see to it myself."

"Great. And I can expect you to send me the prints after the fact?"

"Absolutely."

"Alright, well we're done here. Good luck with Oprah and Debbie. I hear you'll need it." He began to chuckle as he gave his "Good-bye," so I assumed Ms. Dee had bitched about me to him. I'm sure she asked Ahern to nix the booking but that would have put him at odds with his program director, a key exec in his cabinet. *Better to let Oprah do the show than get caught up in the drama that comes with internecine warfare.*

As soon as I was off the line, Lori was back in my office. "Okay for me to walk this memo over to the old man?" We both smiled at her reference for the CEO. I signed it and off it went.

I had done it. Rogers was going to get his wish but as my old man used to say, "Be careful what you wish for, you just might get it."

TRAVELING IN STYLE

It was 5:55 a.m. when the big black limousine pulled up in front of my house. In my right hand I grabbed a suit bag that had two other outfits, shirts, ties, belts and shoes. In my left hand, I picked up my briefcase which had the agenda spelled out for my next three days of publicizing the arrival of Fred Rogers and Mr. Speedy Delivery to Chicago. I was wearing a dark blue suit with stripes, a crisp white shirt and a solid red tie ready to meet the press. But before I could get out the door, I had to say goodbye to Renee. She was up drinking a cup of orange juice as she got set to watch Mister Rogers Neighborhood.

My wife was asleep. Arletta wasn't pleased that I'd literally be gone for the next three days. Oh, I'd see her that Saturday when she brought the kids down for the show, but that would be during a period of high stress for me and Arletta never liked being around me when I was in that kind of mood.

"Daddy, now don't forget –

"Yeah, yeah, Renee, your signed photo and for me to say hi to Mister Rogers. I got it!"

"You better!" She had a determined Shirley Temple look on her face as she crossed her arms to indicate she meant business.

She glowed with an adorable soft pastel pink cotton shade of pale that was comforting to breathe in. I smiled and then bent down to give her a kiss on her forehead. She grabbed the knob and opened the door for me. The limo driver was standing on the porch and immediately stuck his hands out to take my stuff. Renee spotted the long black limo and said, "Wow! That's some car."

I nodded and in my best Mister Rogers voice said. "Yeah Renee, can you spell LIMMM MO ZINE?"

She chuckled at my attempt and shot me a look as if to say – you're off - and then asked, "Is that what it's called."

"Uh huh. Mr. Rogers, Mr. Speedy Delivery and your dad are traveling in style. I got to go – be good to mommy, help her with your little sister and I'll see you tomorrow at the show."

Renee watched me walk down the steps and the walkway to the limo. As I got in, I looked back at her. She gave me a big smile, the kind that filled her face when she was about to giggle and then threw me a kiss. I slapped my cheek as if it had landed. She beamed. It defined dad & daughter and I loved her for it.

About an hour later, I arrived at the Hyatt Regency Hotel in downtown Chicago, a good thirty minutes before the breakfast I had arranged for Fred with Dan Ruth, the critic of the Chicago Sun-Times. David Newell, Mr. McFeely a.k.a. Mr. Speedy Delivery would accompany us on each press interview, but he had made it clear that the focus be on - Mister Rogers.

From a phone call I had received the night before I knew that my Pittsburgh friends had arrived safely at O'Hare and were picked up by the limo driver and on their way to the hotel to check in. What I didn't know was that the Hyatt G.M had upgraded their reservations. His kids loved the show and so he gave Fred and Dave the Presidential Suite at no extra charge. It had a grand staircase that lead to three bedrooms on the second floor. On the first floor, a majestic living room that easily could accommodate 100 guests was blessed with a baby grand piano and a beautiful view of the Chicago River and the iconic architecture of the Wrigley Building and Tribune Tower that hugged the Chicago River.

For the first press interview, I'd make it easy for my brethren from Steeler country. It would be with Dan Ruth, TV critic for the Sun-Times who had literally pleaded with me that as a fan he deserved to get the first interview. I instructed Dan to meet us in the restaurant at the Hyatt on Wacker for breakfast with Mister Rogers at 7:30 a.m. I set it up that way, so my newfound buddies needed to only take an elevator down from the Presidential Suite to the main floor to be in place for what I thought was going to be a softball breakfast interview.

Ruth had called me several weeks before Fred's arrival to ask if I had a ¾ inch videotape screener for an upcoming special he could review. I told him we'd get the screener to him that day via messenger. He then investigated. "Hey, I heard that Fred Rogers is coming to town to help you guys celebrate your 30th anniversary. Is that right?"

"Yeah, we haven't really announced it – but yeah you heard right." I never ever found it smart to be less than completely forthright with a reporter.

Ruth was direct. "I want an interview and I want the first one when he comes to town. I love the guy!"

"Done!" Hell, why wouldn't I give Ruth the first interview? A softball interview would help Fred feel comfortable with Chicago press and that would help make the rest of the day successful. But after about 5 softballs, Dan threw a curve ball that made Fred take a second breath. "I need to know from you

Mister Rogers," Ruth pulled on his taza de café (cup of coffee) and finished it with, "how you feel about Eddie Murphy's characterization of you on Saturday Night Live?"

Fred didn't respond. He tilted his head as if to say, "What?"

Ruth persisted. "You know, when he plays you as Mr. Robinson in Mister Robinson's neighborhood on SNL." The *Mister Robinson* aspect was pure symbolism for urban neighborhood ghetto realism. Fred was either shocked or surprised that Ruth asked the question. He had heard from me that Ruth was a fan, so, this question, which was potentially embarrassing was a turn he didn't expect.

"What do you mean Mr. Ruth?"

"Call me Dan. What I'm trying to find out sir is how you feel about his spoof characterization of you – it's a bit over the top, don't you think?"

I could see how uncomfortable Fred was with the question. I decided to pipe up, "Dan, let's get back to the show, Mister Rogers Neighborhood – we didn't come here to talk about Saturday Night Live."

Dan shot me a look. "Hey Mr. PR, I'm trying to ask a question that many of my readers would probably ask if they had the chance."

Fred looked at me as if to say, "I got this."

"Well, you know what they say Dan, 'imitation is the sincerest form of flattery.'" I was impressed. I hadn't expected such diplomacy but then I really didn't know Fred. We had just met, but I was amazed by Fred's calm and collected answer.

Ruth didn't like the answer. He pressed. "Don't you think Eddie is being just a tad disrespectful?"

Fred didn't bite. He merely shot Ruth a pleasant smile and said, "No. I've never met Eddie but he's a funny man who I don't think means anyone any harm."

Ruth was pissed. He wanted Fred to be forthright, not coy. I was pissed at Dan for pulling his stunt. Don't tell me you love a guy and then try to castrate him.

The rest of the interview didn't go well. Fred was suspicious of Dan from that moment on, which wasn't a good way to start a press tour. In my mind, it was also a harbinger for what Ruth might write. When the article came out, it wasn't the puff piece anyone had hoped for but rather an article critical of Rogers for being a sap and not challenging SNL and Murphy for his caricature. It was only later in time when Dan admitted to me that he might have treated Fred unfairly and if he had it to do over, he would not have written the piece in the manner he did.

Next on the agenda was an appearance with WGN's Roy Leonard. Roy was, at that time, the number one radio talent in his time slot of 10 a.m. to 2 p.m. He was one sweet guy, a prince of a man and an extremely talented storyteller.

Roy's interview of Fred was a press agent's dream. Roy and Fred got along great and the audience phone calls that aired demonstrated the tremendous love people had for Fred, Mr. McFeely, the show, WTTW and public television in general. Roy in his inimitable panache and style found a few nuggets of knowledge that most people never knew about Fred, but somehow Roy uncovered. Roy had a knack for finding that which was unique about his guest and that which his audience might find interestingly amazing. He actually asked a question that I had often wondered myself while watching the program with my daughter Renee. "Fred, why do you talk so slowly?" Fred replied without giving it a thought. "I do that because I'm talking to children. I want them to hear every word I say and to have time to grasp what was said."

Wow, it hit me that perhaps that's why Renee liked the guy so much. She got every bit of what he was trying to communicate.

After finishing with Roy on the radio, we then recorded a short six-minute interview that Robert Jordan of WGN-TV needed to insert into his LIVE coverage package of the stage shows on the upcoming Sunday.

We hopped into our limo at 10:27 a.m. with a "GO-GO-GO" directive to our driver (a cop in real life) – a sharp guy who I figured could somehow get us from the near northwest side to downtown Chicago and ABC7 TV studios within a 30 minute window. A cop can literally get away with anything so making that trip had its moments. Our cop/driver sped down Addison to get us to Lake Shore Drive. Our guy thought nothing of driving on shoulders to move us ahead in the traffic. We arrived at 190 N. State Street, 28 minutes later or in other words on time. I was relieved because I didn't want to hear shit from Debbie about her directive of getting there at 11:00 sharp. My only other major concern was whether Donna and Pat with *Friends of WTTW* corralled those kids and actually had the rug rats in place to see the show. All was good when I heard the receptionist say, "Well the kids certainly won't be disappointed. Hellooooo Mister Rogers!"

The crew was still on lunch. A production assistant welcomed us. That was a message that any seasoned pro in TV would get. Fred Rogers didn't qualify for a producer's greeting – or at least an associate producer's welcome? They sent out a fuckin' P.A.? Really? However, the P.A. kid was genuine and Fred being a nice guy, made a big deal about the young man having a job in a network-owned and operated TV station in a major market like Chicago. The kid lit up. You could see that Fred had somehow touched the P.A. – so pleased to hear Mister Rogers cherished him. The P.A. wanted Fred ready as quickly as possible. He mentioned prior to stepping out the door, "Sir, ah…Mister Rogers…Oprah and the Executive Producer, will stop by to go over a few things prior to rolling tape – not to worry - standard–operating–procedure." Fred nodded and thanked the young man.

ANYTHING BUT STANDARD OPERATING PROCEDURE

The scene of the meet and greet between Fred Rogers and Oprah Winfrey would be perhaps worthy of insertion into a William Shakespeare farce like -*The Taming of the Shrew*. There was a heavy knock on the door of the GREEN ROOM, which then opened without waiting for a "come in," command from the guest. It was Oprah followed by Debbie. They literally walked straight towards Fred and me. David was seated to our left in a comfortable chair reading a magazine and didn't initially notice Oprah's presence until conversation broke the air in that room. Noticing that Debbie wasn't about to open her mouth, I extended my hand and began to say, "Hi Oprah, I'm –

Oprah cut me off with a wave of her hand. "Oh, I know who you are!" She then turned her gaze to Fred. "Hello Fred." Fred smiled at Oprah, extended his hand, which Oprah accepted and said, "It's so good to finally meet you Oprah." WOW. I didn't expect what came next but hell it had been like that all day, so why not?

Oprah gave Fred a look that if you could put into a translator would come back at you in garbled computer speech as: "What'dya talkin' about motherfucker?" Oprah didn't express that thought audibly but Fred immediately knew he had said the wrong thing. "You don't remember me - do you Fred?" Fred's eyes went vacant of any color for a split second. He was torn. He didn't want to say the wrong thing again. He remained silent with a look that via the translator would have revealed itself as, "I haven't got a fuckin' clue regarding what you're talking about Oprah." Oprah shook her head and said, "Fred, we've met. It was about 10 years ago and I interviewed you on camera while you were visiting Baltimore." Fred probably should have invoked SILENCE, but I think he truly didn't remember and wanted to express his apology. "I'm so sorry, I don't recall going into a Baltimore TV station." She cut him off. "We did the interview on the street – you answered three questions for me."

That's how it started, and we were still in the GREEN ROOM. Oprah turned and said, "See you on the set." She walked out with Debbie following her. As the door shut, Fred looked at me for my reaction. My reaction wasn't any different than that of David's. We were all in shock. But within moments an A-2 audio technician was putting a wireless microphone pack on Fred. The floor manager came in next and Fred was whisked to the set. I found myself standing by the huge white studio doors looking at an audience of kids mixed with a few moms and dads eager to greet Mister Rogers. To my left was Ms. Debbie Dee, the Executive Producer, closest to the set, then me, then the wife of the General Manager known simply as, "Mrs. Ahern."

Towards the end of the show, Mrs. Ahern leaned out and over me to look at Debbie without moving from her spot. "You know Debbie. I'm making Joe his favorite dinner - Irish beef stew. He deserves it – the kids are ecstatic!" Deb didn't really do much other than smile. Mrs. Ahern continued, "Debbie, you should be proud. This is the best show you've ever produced!" Debbie was shocked, but she nodded a look of thanks. I then leaned over to Debbie, "Damn, there's a feather in your cap."

Debbie didn't say anything - but she did mouth a "Fuck you," that only my eyes could see.

At the conclusion of the show, the kids rushed the stage and Oprah struck a pose that I can only describe as "perplexed." Fred was having a blast with the kids surrounding him. The credit role took only about a minute and then we heard the floor director announce, "All clear!"

The consensus in the limo was that despite the discomfort of the GREEN ROOM meeting with Oprah (for a second time), Winfrey did her homework and conducted a solid interview about the status of children's television and the people who make it. I surmised that the adulation Fred got from the kids and their parents made his spirit soar. Fred had hoped that Oprah would reappear to say goodbye, but that never happened. It was the young P.A. who with a bit of a smile in his voice told us, "Oprah has left the building."

Our limo driver took us north up the Magnificent Mile for a late lunch at the swanky Spiaggia Ristorante with Tribune TV critic, Rick Kogan. Rick, like Roy, loved Fred, the show and the mission of children's TV in the hands of a quality producer who could not only entertain but also teach. Rick had a deadline, so upon concluding his interview he headed back to the Trib.

We borrowed a phone brought to the table that the waiter plugged in. We then conducted two quick interviews over the phone with critics in daily papers with smaller circulations before heading back to WTTW for an interview with John Calloway of Chicago Tonight. It was on this ride, that Fred suggested I take a quick nap. I looked at him, smiled and said, "Sir, a publicist doesn't take naps when they're working for a client." Fred nodded and said, "We're in the car, there's nothing more we can expect of you till we arrive. C'mon - take a nap." I was in no mood to argue so I did lean my head back, closed my eyes and began to realize that this guy – this Fred Rogers - was the real deal – as nice in person as he was on TV.

When we got to WTTW, we took Fred and Dave immediately to say hello to Mr. William (Bill) McCarter, the CEO who as it happened had John Calloway in his office. John would be interviewing Fred for his show, Chicago Tonight. McCarter wanted to also emphasize the importance of having Fred record a TV announcement for the upcoming pledge marketing effort. McCarter thanked Fred for his willingness to help WTTW celebrate its 30th Anniversary.

As a member of the WTTW family, I was still new to the incessant need by public TV to ask viewers to pay for what they got for free over the airways after the fact. WTTW was also one of only 10 public TV stations in the country at that time allowed to broadcast commercials. That test would eventually prove so successful that PTV stations throughout the country were granted the ability to do the same by the Federal Communications Commission (FCC). The third point that McCarter wanted to share with Fred was a bit of background on who would be in the audience that evening at a dinner of 650 benefactors. The Deputy Mayor planned on attending the dinner along with various alderman and notable WTTW board members and advisors who were multi-millionaires – possibly billionaires - like Lester and Renee Crown and Gordon Segal of Crate & Barrel fame.

The taped interview for that evening's presentation of Chicago Tonight couldn't have been smoother. Fred was safe with Calloway who focused on Fred's career and his contribution to quality programs directed specifically towards child development. John and his producers had a video of Mr. Roger's appeal before Congress in 1969 when he gave an emotional plea to Senator Pastore, a member of a Senate Subcommittee that was considering whether to continue or cut government funding for public television. Nixon was trying to eliminate funding for PBS. Mr. Rogers was trying to save it. Fred was convinced that he offered an expression of care on every episode to help each child watching realize that they were special – that they were unique.

Pastore was so impressed by Rogers that he allowed him to actually recite the lyrics of a song that Fred wrote and performed on the show that went, "What do you do with the mad that you feel?" Fred noted that that first line came from a child. He continued with a repeat of the first line and just kept going. "What, do you do with the mad that you feel? When you feel so mad that you could bite? When the whole wide world seems oh so wrong, and nothing you do seems very right. What, do you do? Do you punch a bag? Do you pound some clay or some dough? Do you round up friends for a game of tag or see how fast you go? It's great to be able to stop, when you've planned the thing that's wrong. And be able to do something else instead - and think this song. I can stop when I want to and stop when I wish and stop, stop, stop anytime. And what a good feeling to feel like this and know that feeling is really mine - know that there's something deep inside that helps us become what we can, for a girl can be someday a lady and a boy can be someday a man." Pastore, a rather gruff character flashed a huge smile and said, "I think it's wonderful. I think it's wonderful. Looks like you just earned the twenty million dollars." Instead of cutting the budget, the Senate instead increased the budget given to PBS. That was an awesome clip for John and his staff to have dug up for playback in that interview.

Damn - our limo driver was good. Even with the late afternoon crush of traffic congestion, he got us back to the Hyatt on Wacker

Drive by 7:15 p.m. That allowed us time to get ready for the 8 p.m. dinner in the ballroom on the hotel's second floor. I had my change of clothes in the limo. Fred's suite had three full bathrooms, so all of us, Fred, David and I were able to take a shower and get changed into a set of fresh clothes for the upcoming banquet.

David and I were ready by 7:45 p.m. David had parked himself at the grand piano whose flap was up. He was playing something classical and it sounded good. Fred had to return a few calls, so I figured he'd need a few more minutes but I was sure we'd make it down to the second floor by 8 p.m. I had been checking my watch constantly as the sun went down. It was still summer albeit late in the season; we were blessed with a bit of light bouncing off the glass of the downtown buildings.

The phone rang at 7:53 p.m. and I was sure it was Mr. McCarter demanding that I get the man of honor down to the ballroom. Instead it was my daughter Renee.

"Hi Daddy. Is Mister Rogers there?"

"Renee, what are you doing up? You should be in bed. Let me talk to Mommy."

"Mommy is down in the basement doing laundry. I asked her if I could talk to you and Mister Rogers and she said, 'Sure, why not?'"

I realized my wife was not happy that I failed to call home. I should have but when I worked for a client - I was in a zone. My failure to call at times earned me a cold shoulder when I crossed the threshold after a long day of publicity. I should have followed Fred's example because he made a point of telling me he needed to check how his wife was doing. In the course of the day, Fred asked me about my family, so he knew I was married and had two small children.

The call from Renee was not only notification of my wife's frustration but also her way of pissing me off. She knew

I couldn't blow Renee off and would find the intrusion disconcerting. Yeah, I was driven - but that's why I had a rep as a premier publicist - because of my focus.

"Listen Renee, I got to go, I'm working."

I could see David staring at me through the opening of the flap of the grand piano he played. He shook his head as if to let me know something was awry.

"Daddy – daddy, please let me talk to Mister Rogers."

"No way!"

"Why not? And did you get that photo for me?"

"Hey…

Now David's head was like a bobble doll – spinning disapproval.

"I told you I'd get you a photo of Mister Rogers, now stop bugging-

I abruptly ground to a halt when I felt someone tapping my shoulder. David had stopped playing. His face was turning white as if the blood had drained out of it.

I turned and it was Fred who immediately burst out, "Who are you talking to?"

"Ah…well it's my-

"Is it a child?"

"Yes sir. It's my daughter."

"Give me that phone!"

Fred literally yanked the phone from my hands. He let a second lapse and then announced, "Hi, this is Mister Rogers. Who is this?"

Fred literally turned his back to me as he continued. "Ah, Reneeeeee. Yes, your dad told me about you, and I understand that you and your sister...is it Gina?" He listened for a moment. "Ah, I got it right. I remember your dad telling me you're a big sister." He listened. "7 and a half. Yes, that definitely makes you the big sister."

I looked at my watch. It was now 7:58 and I needed Fred to get off the phone so I positioned myself so that I could hold my wrist out and point to the time on my watch. Fred ignored me and David looked as if he was about to have a heart attack. I didn't get it. We needed to be downstairs in two minutes and we needed to leave now. Fred continued his conversation. "I'm looking forward to it too and yes, King Friday, Henrietta Pussycat and Lady Elaine will be with me. I understand you watch the show every morning."

It was now 8:01 and we were late, so I pointed again to my watch, only to have Fred turn away. He continued to talk with Renee for another three minutes finally concluding the call by saying, "Well Renee, would you like to talk with your dad?" Fred listened. "Oh, no? You don't want to? Well, goodbye Renee. It was a pleasure talking with you."

Fred bent down to hang up the phone gently. He then stood up straight and after looking at David for a moment he turned to me and with a bit of blood in his eye said. "Look, you seem like a nice young guy BUT let's get something straight since we'll be together for the next two days." He waited for me to acknowledge him, which I did with a nod of my head.

"You will never interrupt me when I'm talking to a child, even if that child is your own." Fred waited for me to react but all I could do was lower my eyes and whisper, "Yes sir."

"Okay. Now let's get downstairs. I'm starving. How about you young man?"

It was that quick. He had made his point and then all seemed forgiven. He was right. I was abrupt with my daughter and for what?

We headed down to the ballroom and even though we were about ten minutes late, no one seemed to mind. They all wanted to meet the man. They were mesmerized by his mission that children be encouraged to aspire to become whatever they dreamed of being in life.

It was a long day but a beautiful one as Fred's lyrics filled my soul with a bit of hope for me. "Won't you be mine, could you be mine, won't you be my neighbor?"

And what a neighbor he proved to be. Fred had insisted that of the 2500 in attendance for his stage productions, 250 seats had to be set aside gratis for children with disabilities. Instead of taking a break between shows, Fred met with each of the kids with special needs. He had a conversation with every child as rich as the one he had shared with Renee. At one point from a distance of about 50 feet, I could swear I saw an aura of colors and a pleasant shade of pale surrounding the outline of a man I began to view as divine.

My kids each got a chance to meet Fred and Mr. McFeely who at one point held Gina in his arms. My wife loved meeting Fred and her cold shoulder warmed towards me. She saw how devoted I had become to the man and his vocation that I had initially rejected. It was, for all of us, a blessing to have a guy like Fred Rogers in our neighborhood because he made our lives richer with his presence. What more can anyone want from a neighbor? Each conversation, each touch, each embrace, each smile was precious. For me the greatest gift I got from Mister Rogers that weekend was learning to live in the moment.

TWO YEARS LATER

The speakers crashed the terminal with a feedback that then broke clearly. "Attention all passengers on Delta Flight 3205 from Chicago to Hartsfield Airport. Delta welcomes you to Atlanta! Your baggage has been sent to Carousel B…that's a change from what was posted. Please note that luggage from Delta 3205 will be at Carousel B. Thank you."

I was off to the Broadcast Promotion & Marketing Executives (BPME) association annual conference, which attracted marketing professionals, television producers pushing their specials, syndicators doing the same with their reruns, their game and talk shows, which invariably included the folks at HARPO. By now - *The Oprah Winfrey Show* was shortened to *Oprah*. Everybody in the U.S. knew who Oprah was. She was bound for global brand status and got it. Eventually her syndication guys - KING WORLD - would book the show into numerous countries worldwide.

I had been the chairman of the BPME in 1985 when WTTW hired me away from NBC. One of my conditions was that Window To The World Communications – the parent company, cover my membership to the BPME, my travel for BPME Board Meetings and my attendance at the annual conference which could be anywhere in the 50 states.

I spotted my bag moving towards me on Carousel B. The luggage was fairly large since my stay in Atlanta required four nights and three days of my time. I had to give my luggage one hell of a yank to get it over the border of the carousel and wound up turning my body away from the exit doors and towards the wall the carousel ran along. Directly in front of me was the back of a woman who was struggling to get her large bag off of the carousel. I took four steps forward. Without me saying anything I put my hand over hers, she let go of the handle and I pulled the bag up and over that carousel curb. During this move I was so concerned of bringing the bag down without it landing on anyone's feet that I didn't notice the woman had turned to me while I was in a bent over shape. As I straightened up, I immediately recognized the woman and said, "Hi Debbie, how you doing? Long time since we talked."

Now by this time Debbie was making big bucks. As the Exec Producer of a top-rated syndication show she was easily pulling 6 figures plus, plus, plus and maybe even 7 figures since the Harpo production was #1 nationwide in talk - it was beating the long-time KING of TALK – Donahue. So maybe some of that had all gone to her head because the rest of the exchange surprised me.

Debbie shook her head. "I don't think we've ever met. Nevertheless, thank you sir for helping me."

"What? 'Thank you, sir, for helping me?' You're kidding-right. Debbie - you know me."

She gave me a look as if she was taking me in from my penny loafers to my sports coat, tie/shirt combination and then focusing on my eyeballs said, "Sir, again many thanks, but no, I don't know you."

I shook my head in disbelief. She waited for me to move so she could steer her luggage toward the doors. She probably wasn't taking a taxi. She probably had a car waiting for her, perhaps a limo. I couldn't help myself and said, "Okay, well maybe this will help. I'm the guy who shoved Mister Rogers up your ass. Remember me?"

She turned into CAT WOMAN and above the hiss I could hear quite clearly, "FUCK YOU PR Hack!!"

I smiled. "So, you do remember me." I turned, grabbed my bag and like many a promotion guy I went towards the sunset never to see my adorable Debbie-D again.

16 YEARS LATER

"Hmm – one gets butter on the bread before the peanut butter and jelly is spread…and one doesn't – but which one goes into which lunch pail?" I was known to talk to myself early in the morning when making lunches for Matt and Carissa.

Renee was 13 years older than Matt and 8 years older than Carissa. Gina was 5 years minus on both of those numbers. She may have been the second oldest daughter but when she was in the room with the eldest, you'd never consider Renee to be her senior. Gina had an overpowering presence about her. She was also the tallest of all the kids.

Renee was off on her own teaching first graders at a Chicago Public School in Chicago. She was out of the house and had her own condo with a bit of help from her parents. Gina was off at college.

My day usually began at 5 a.m. I had been getting up early to go to work as a TV director for news that required that I report at 4 a.m. So, on my days when I wasn't scheduled, I decided it might be best to stick to the schedule. I tried to make the little ones their lunches. I'd also clean up the kitchen a bit and then make breakfast for them when they reported to the kitchen. I often had the radio set to WBBM-AM-NEWSRADIO 78 to catch the early morning newscast.

"This just in on WBBM News-radio 78 – there is a report, sad to say, that Fred Rogers of Mister Rogers Neighborhood passed away last night at his home with his wife by his side in the city he loved, Pittsburgh. We'll bring you more details as they come in…and now it's time for Sports." A sports fanfare of horns filled the air. I turned off the radio. I picked up the house phone and called Renee.

Ring–ring-ring-ring-ring. "C'mon Renee pick it up." I continued to talk to myself over more rings. And then I heard a click.

"Okay dad, this better be good. Who died?" I was amazed and a bit confused that she responded that way.

"What?"

"Who died? You know I'm up getting ready for school but c'mon dad – you never call me at this hour. I almost wasn't going to pick it up…so who died?"

"Oh, yeah. You've got caller ID."

"Yeah – c'mon – who died?"

"Well actually nobody. Uh, NO – I don't really mean that. No one in the family has died if that's what you mean?"

"Well then who?"

"You're not going to like it, but I just heard that Mister Rogers passed away during the night."

The phone seemed to go dead. I wasn't sure if the connection was still good. And then I heard it. Renee was weeping. Not a wailing kind of weep but a tender, soft cry that was filled with a breath of sadness. I couldn't help but ask?

"Hey Pumpkin, you okay?"

"Yeah dad. I'll be okay but that's awful. You know I loved the man and his show. You remember?"

"How could I forget that – especially after he chastised me for how I talked with you when you called his hotel room."

"God bless Mister Rogers. You had that coming dad!" There was joy in her voice and I didn't care if it was at my expense. Renee never had a problem of telling her father the truth.

"Yeah, and if I could have that moment all over again, I wouldn't want it any different. I learned a lot from the man, and I learned a bit from you as well, Pumpkin. I never told you but eventually I became a fan of the show."

"Well, thanks for sharing. Were you planning on taking that one to your grave dad – wait – don't answer that! I really have to go dad. I'll say a little prayer for Fred and a big one for you! Love you!"

That made my day! I was at peace with Fred transitioning because he was just such a good man. It was only natural for me to hum/sing a few bars as the rug rats awoke and came down for breakfast. "*It's a beautiful day in* this *neighborhood. Won't you be mine, could you be mine, won't you please be my neighbor.*" They both smiled. Dad was in a good mood. It was a great day for all!

THE REST OF THE STORY

In my career, I have been fortunate to work for some truly outstanding broadcasters including Paul Harvey, who at one time had a radio program on over 250 radio stations in the U.S. Harvey was on WGN in Chicago. He was a national treasure who at 90 was signed by the ABC Radio Network to a ten-year contract at ten million dollars a year. His son, Paul Aurandt, was a multi-talented individual. He reveled as a musical composer and as a brilliant storyteller who wrote all of the scripts for "The Rest of the Story," a feature of the syndicated Paul Harvey Report. I loved "The Rest of the Story," because it was the unexpected. A tease recited prior to the commercial break intended to pique your interest and get you to come back was part of the feature. The one I remember the most was so unique and intrigued even me, an avowed history buff. Paul Harvey asked the audience if they could name the occupant of the White House who had been a spousal abuser. I couldn't imagine who that president was. It turned out to be Mary Todd and her penchant for often hitting her hubby who we all knew as Honest Abe.

So, what was "The Rest of the Story," to this saga of Mr. Rogers?

Around 10:30 on the same morning I called Renee to inform her of Fred's passing, I got a call in my office at home from a producer at WTTW. She wondered if I would be kind enough to help her with leads to secure possible guests for a special show that evening on Chicago Tonight which would focus an entire half-hour of their hour – remembering all things Mister Rogers. She asked me if I could possibly give her three names of professionals in the Chicago area that had a connection to Mister Rogers. The young woman was aware that I had worked at WTTW and spent three days with Fred when he had come to Chicago some 18 years earlier.

I had to roll through my Rolodex but within moments I gave her names and phone numbers of prominent people in Chicago that Fred had interacted with and knew. The first name I suggested was the president of the Central Educational Network who had been instrumental in getting Fred's show exposure regionally and then nationally. The second guest was a child psychologist who had been called upon by Fred for advice and counsel when they tackled delicate childhood subjects. The third was a director/producer who had worked on Fred Rogers' specials – different from the daily shows. All three lived in the Chicago area. Each person I recommended; I knew professionally and/or personally. I was confident they'd make a great line-up. She then asked me if I could watch the show and then share with her a critique. I feigned being too busy. Frankly, that was a no-win situation for me. If I criticized any one of the guests and my remarks somehow got back to them, I'd be putting my relationship in jeopardy. I didn't need that and so I politely told her as much as I'd like to help, I just couldn't find the time.

She then asked if I had any kind of an anecdote to share about Fred. I told her, "No, but I can tell you what happened this morning at 5 a.m. with my daughter, Renee, who met Mister Rogers and fell in love with him." The associate producer took a beat before she responded. I figured she just wanted to be polite as she blew me off, so I was amazed when she said, "I'd love to hear more about that."

At the time of the WTTW call, I was working freelance as a camera operator, a director, a writer and a producer. When I left permanent employment, I was afraid of what the future held. But I didn't give myself enough credit. I had a lot of talents and although I wasn't picture perfect at any of my marketable skills, I was a consummate professional who sought to give 100% to any project assigned to my care. My dance card was full. I had more work than I knew what to do with. I worked long days. I ended the call politely but insistent that I truly didn't have the leisure of being a TV critic.

But on that same day when I called Renee in the wee hours to tell her of the loss of a good man, I found myself swamped dealing with what I hated the most - the paperwork demands of invoicing those I worked for as an independent contractor and freelancer. Imagine my curiosity when my office phone rang and from caller ID, I could tell that it was WTTW for the second time that day contacting me. That's when I heard a voice under stress. It was the young associate producer I had spoken with earlier that day. "Say, can you make it to the WTTW studios by 6:30?"

"Why?"

"Ah, because one of the three guests you gave us, had to pull out at the last minute due to a medical emergency."

"I'm sorry to hear that but you do realize that it's now 5:20 p.m. and you're asking me to travel 35 miles during rush hour traffic from Downers Grove to the near northwest side of Chicago…that's going to be hard to do."

"Could you try? if I don't find someone…."

I knew what that pressure felt like when I produced programming and had somebody cut out on me at the last minute;

I'd be upset too. "Okay, I'll try and make it, but I won't get there till 6:55 p.m. So have the audio tech ready to mic me up at the last minute – but if he's any good, it's not a big deal."

"That's great and please try to get here even a few minutes before that if you can."

"Not going to happen. Now I have to go if I'm going to make 6:55 and I'm telling you to be forewarned, my ten-year old boy comes with me. I've got no one to watch him. His mom and his sister are out tonight for an event at school."

"We normally don't allow kids, but I'm sure it'll be fine under the circumstances."

As predicted, my son and I got to WTTW at 6:55 p.m. We were immediately ushered into the GREEN ROOM for guests when a man I had worked with at NBC5, a news writer and some-times on-air sportscaster by the name of Mike appeared on the scene. He was introduced by the associate producer, the young lady I spoke with on the phone, as the new supervising producer for Chicago Tonight. It became clear to the young woman that I needed no introduction when Mike commented, "Well, look what the cat dragged in?"

I shot a look at the man and then said quietly between us, "Enough Mike, my boy is with me. No matter what our differences from our days at NBC, don't do that in front of a kid, otherwise I'm walking out." Mike quickly shut up. A tech put a mic on me and then took me to the floor director who directed me where to sit.

John Calloway had retired. Calloway's replacement as the anchor was Phil Ponce, an alumnus of ABC7.

I was pleased that the second half of the hour was going to be all about Mister Rogers and that Phil would conduct the discussion and then close out the show. My only complaint was that I was told to rush to WTTW when in fact I could have been accorded the respect of being granted more time to deal with traffic on my way to the studio. However, I also know how anxious producers are about having their guests locked down and in place on a set. Even though I was a TV professional who would have known when and where to walk in a hot studio, I don't think that reality was on the minds of the producers or if it was, not something they wanted the crew to have to deal with.

Two of the three guests I suggested were with me as we waited for the first half of the show to play out. The president of the Central Education TV Network (CEN) located in Des Plaines (a Chicago suburb), was on my right. That gentleman made it possible for the program, *Mister Rogers Neighborhood*, to be broadcast on the Midwest regional affiliates of CEN. That exposure convinced PBS to carry it nationwide. CEN PREZ had a wonderful working relationship with Fred and had dinner with him on several occasions, which allowed him to get to know one of the best TV professionals in the business when it came to producing programming for children.

The woman to my left was a child psychologist that had served as advisor to the show regarding all questions about the psychology of children. She had spoken several times by phone with Fred and knew of his passion to effectively and accurately communicate with children in the hope of helping them understand their feelings, be they glad, sad, mad or even bad.

I was stuck in the middle between them. Phil was to our right at the end of the table on the set. I made a point to myself that I would listen more than talk. After all, the other two guests were professionals that had worked with Fred for years. I spent roughly 72 hours with him. But I did answer any question Phil posed to me directly like, "What was your initial impression of Mister Rogers?"

I hesitated and Phil sensed it. "It's okay, take your time. Just share with our public what you shared with our producer."

"Hmmm. Well, if I'm perfectly honest Phil, I did not like the show and as a result didn't care much for the man."

"Anddddd??? What changed your mind?"

I shared the story about Fred encouraging me to take a nap while we traveled in the limousine. "That's unheard of! And even though I worked for WTTW at that time, he was our client. He was just that damn nice."

Phil began posing questions to the other guests. I remember thinking - *Good, don't ask me anything else. Focus on the others.*

When I noticed a camera change via the tally lights on the cameras and realized that I wasn't up on the wide shot, I stole a peak at my watch and noticed that there was a mere 3 minutes left in show. That's when a bomb hit.

Phil looked at me and said, "You told our producer about your call this morning at 5 a.m. with your daughter revealing the passing of her fan favorite, Mister Rogers."

" I know it sounds strange but I had to share with Renee, my Pumpkin as I call her, of the news I just heard via a radio station noting the passing of Mister Rogers in his hometown of Pittsburgh, Pennsylvania with his wife by his side."

"Did your daughter Renee get a chance to meet Mister Rogers?" Phil looked awfully smart in that double-breasted suit and very much like an attorney who knew the answer to his question.

That's all I could think of as I answered. "Oh yes, she met him backstage at one of his puppet-shows that he performed that weekend back in '85 at the Auditorium in celebration of WTTW's 30th Anniversary. Renee was a huge fan of Mister

Rogers and the show and even spoke with him for several minutes on the phone."

"That's what I want you to share with our viewers. Please tell that story."

Upon concluding my story, Phil smiled and looked straight into his close-up camera and said, "How appropriate to end this special segment of Mister Rogers with a real, true story of what the man was like, what he expected of adults when dealing with children, whether they were your own or not. Thank you, for sharing that.

And I want to thank my panel." Phil then went on to elucidate the names of the other two guests and bid the viewers a good night.

As the credits rolled over video of Phil and his guests on set in the studio, the audio man played over the studio PA and out to broadcast land, a song which at one time I hated and now had fondness for its empathetic shade of pale, "Could you be mine? Would you be mine? Please won't you be my neighbor?"

Where Was Rumpelstiltskin When You Needed Him?

Mary Denise had returned to her old digs at NBC as a freelance TV news and promotion director. As a Marketing & Promotion producer, I often worked with her.

"Mary Denise was a fox…and not necessarily only in her looks but also in the way she carried herself…a quality once expected of any lady but in the time frame we were in, that was often overlooked. She had an air about her that was very New England."

Two young girls found her not only cosmopolitan but attractive and yet a woman who knew her way around horses, something she shared with those girls…a chance to ride on a pony without the stupid CARNY counting down the seconds you had to dismount. Last but hardly least, MD lived in the LOOP and the kids thought that was the bomb. My ex, Arletta, didn't seem to mind. She was into some new guy.

But MD couldn't get the guy she had lived with for the last three years out of her head. He promised to marry her. The guy was loaded, and I mean loaded. He was a bit older by about 12 to 15 years, but age was and is nothing more than a number when you're in love - or think you are especially if the prize exudes youth in spite of the shading of FATHER TIME. The man provided a very comfortable life in a huge, some might label, mansion style abode. They traveled all over the world. Life was good.

But it wasn't any of that.

What it was…simply put - came down to one word, "R-E-S-P-E-C-T!"

Oh, my goodness! When had I become so sensitive? Had I turned gay?

Mr. Money Bags gave his trophy credibility when he introduced her to everyone as his fiancé. That was great in the beginning, but, lost its luster after year three.

Of course, an ultimatum was decreed for the sanctity of the woman's honor. That eventually put the nail in the coffin and MD was back as a working stiff rather than maintaining a madam of leisure lifestyle.

It was Mr. Money Bags who did the dumping as the wind cried for Mary.

If he indicated even the slightest hint that he'd take her back, she was there for the picking. That might sound harsh but not as harsh as the way that man manipulated an otherwise very competent, self-assured woman and when I say woman…I mean a woman who had it all, great looks, a great education, a great family (at times) and a swagger that only melted around Mr. Money Bags.

Sans Money Bags, MD was looking for a bit of adventure minus the commitment. Most men would have found that acceptable but I'm not most men.

What could have been a torrid love affair was more like friends with benefits. Once that had been established, I made it known I'd always be there in need, but I needed some space and I intended to move on.

"As long as you're there when I call." She smiled with wide open eyes.

I couldn't say NO to those foxy green eyes. I merely nodded knowing that we would eventually become ships passing in the night. And that's exactly what happened. I did move on and she moved back in with Mr. Money Bags.

Several months later, I met a former female NBC colleague at a NATAS – National Academy of Television Arts & Sciences award ceremony. We hit it off quickly and within three months we were engaged with a wedding to follow set for a little over seven months later.

It was during those seven months…and I can't remember how far in I was on the 7, when a woman caller came calling for me at my place of work about Noon one day.

I was pleasantly surprised to see MD. "Have you had lunch yet?" I asked.

She smiled and shook her head NO as her eyes radiated an aura of green that encased me with the mystique that a foxy woman can have on a man.

There was a Chinese restaurant down the street that despite its tiny size knew how to cook Cantonese to perfection.

"I've got some news for you." MD smiled as she looked across the table at me while we awaited our orders.

"And I've got some news for you!" As colleagues, we had remained good friends in spite of what little romance there was; because it was mainly physical, albeit *great physical* – that woman was ZEN when it came to her yoga moves. BUT let's face it, we both still cared a great deal about each other. That's why we had turned into excited little kids willing to share our secrets after missing each other's presence for several months. Several months where something could happen and did.

I was selfish. I wanted to go first.

I shared the news of my nuptials. That was obviously a SIGN that she hadn't expected. Her face became RED - filled with blood. It was only then that I knew I had walked into a perfect MESS.

She explained that she and Mr. Money Bags were completely and finally history that would never be revisited. She had to see me to tell me. She wanted us to move ahead as more than friends with benefits but rather lovers. It was almost as if she hadn't heard a word I said. There was no question that we did love one another. BUT there was just the constant advent that the swash buckling debonair Cary Grant Mr. Money Bags would always make us at best a threesome with MD switching partners again and again.

"Timing is everything Mary. Be happy for me. I am in love with the woman, you know her."

Yes, MD did know her. They fortunately had never had a conflict or an issue so it wasn't as if MD could bad mouth my choice or give me a reason or show me a sign why my intentions weren't solid…as solid as anybody's rationale or logic or calculus can be when it comes to LOVE. You know IT when you're in IT. IT is a shade of pale that is pure bliss that sure beats a bullet in the head.

Fortunately, in this tale, there was no perfect crime and I had a reason to live and LOVE without fear of feeling the tragedy of a woman scorned. If anything, I had been the victim. She had sent me away with her quest to have it all. Sometimes you get money, lots of it. Sometimes you get LOVE, lots of it. But you rarely get both shades of pale. It was a gamble and I couldn't blame her for her choices but unfortunately for MD the fairytale she had prayed for never came through and Rumpelstiltskin didn't bother to show up to turn straw into gold.

As to my gold, well let's just say that with time it turned into pewter.

Ah LOVE, it fills you up, tosses you upside down and then extracts the blood that an unlawful carnal affair can claim on your soul when your beloved disappoints you…a sin against LOVE even if LOVE, albeit forbidden, had everything to do with it.

After years being apart, we did run away together to commiserate about our failed romances over beer and music in Austin, Texas. We heard the tunes of Sir Paul McCartney and ate the best TEX/MEX anyone could ever hope for. But we had both moved on in so many ways that to consider that we would experience bliss from a weekend that would somehow transcend the 2400 miles between us literally and emotionally was too much of a fairytale even if Rumpelstiltskin had promised to turn that straw into a gold shade of pale that called out for more.

Adriana's Email

Sometimes love comes in the form of an email that may not bring bliss but nevertheless provides a panacea for a wounded spirit.

The exchange was to confirm a dinner date on next month's calendar for Adriana, her husband and me. I met Adriana's husband, Jim, before I met her; but during the inaugural reception by both man and wife, I felt incredibly comfortable and able to unwind as if WE had known each other all our lives. When you run into a person, in this case for me, persons, who make you feel like you're sitting down to a dinner of golden dumplings…you've got to admit that's COMFORTING COMFORT FOOD.

With Jim, it started by me hiring the man to be an instructor at a vocational college, where I served as the Executive Director or BOSS MAN, which featured a curriculum for BROADCAST MEDIA ARTS. The word spread quickly and in very short time, Jim became the most popular instructor at the school.

I was lucky to forge a friendship with Jim. He was incredibly talented as an editor and a photographer of still or moving pictures, but more importantly, the man glowed with a shade of pale that was so inviting. It was as blue as the sea and the sky and the sky and the sea whipped together…easy on the eyes, easy on the mind. AND – he was incredibly PATIENT…a gift from God because PATIENCE was required when dealing with novices. Some novices, but a rare few indeed, had the *eye* – as either an editor or a shooter. But when you got one like that, Jim knew how to make the most of that diamond in the rough.

After Jim left as an instructor at the school, we stayed in touch which lead to me being asked to be on the founding board of a 501c3 that would work with indigent youth to develop an interest in photography and software platform electronic editing. Jim called it *SHINE ON CHICAGO.*

Adriana was also on the board and so that's how we all came together for what we all viewed as a worthwhile charitable effort. The board meetings sometimes could be fun, like the night we had one at the friendly confines of Wrigley Field, home of our beloved CUBS courtesy of Adriana and Jim. And if we were just having a regular like board meeting, we had it at Jim & Adriana's but always after dinner was served first …usually deep-dish-pizza, salad, and wine. The dinners were a great way for all of us to get to know one another, and that included the other board members.

The dinners made us feel like family. Funny how getting a number of people around a table of food can do that.

So, I was touched when I read in addition to a confirmation of our dinner date a thought wave that hit me in my gut core even if it was only in PRINT:

> *"Also, Jim and I noticed you were not yourself when we saw you last and it's probably due to Matt's anniversary coming up. Please know that we care about you and if you need company our door is always open."*

Yes, the anniversary was coming up. A day I had learned to HATE, and I had always promised myself I would never HATE, but HATE I did for that DATE. The DATE when my son took his life by his own hand. OH, that DATE elicited HATE from me. Why? Why? On my last breath I'll be asking Why?

We only met for moments. I was returning a book they had loaned me. But Adriana saw it and so did Jim. It was one of my BLUE days. Those BLUE days had obviously become obvious. I'd hear a song on the radio, maybe one that didn't even have much to do with Matt and yet trigger in me my captain, oh captain of a ship with all hands-on deck sailing on a course unknown to man into a sea of BLUE. Tears were often draining out of my eyes as my face felt the warmth of that rain. And speaking of rain, I often suffered that BLUE Moon of a day at the sound of James Taylor singing FIRE & RAIN. Maybe because that song did light up the elephants in the room: suicide, heroin addiction and mental health gasping in a mental health hospital. All of that FIRE & RAIN landed on my son, God love him! I know I did!

What was incredibly comforting were the words that followed. The announcement that my pain was a shade of pale that was so overwhelming it couldn't help but be noticed.

I read the WORDS of Adriana's email, over and over. Those WORDS carried a weight much heavier than TALK, because we all know that TALK is CHEAP, and I didn't have to worry about that with a couple that were so worthy of my trust. The WORDS were just so, just so friggin' COMFORTABLE!

"Please know that we care about you and if you need company our door is always open."

Oh my God! What BLISS!

"…we care about you…"

"…our door is always open."

And I got all misty eyed from an email…a very short email…and yet the effect on me was anything but SHORT. I was verklempt; I mean it. I didn't know what to think.

I was still BLUE but at least it was a cozy BLUE. I hated being BLUE because it made me feel COLD. COLD was what my son was and damn it, he should have had many more seasons of Spring, Summer, Fall and Winter. He loved Winter the most, so I prayed he didn't mind being COLD. Maybe he was where he was supposed to be even if I couldn't figure it out.

Why so young? That was the toughest part. But the time he had, was wisely chosen by his parents. He traveled the world. He laughed and laughed while he put his music to your troubles or HIS so you could dance them all away. He loved being a DJ.

Not only was the day not far from the anniversary of his departure, the State of Illinois Revenue Department had sent a letter which I opened earlier demanding payment of parking fines owed with the power of withholding dollars from any upcoming tax refund. I wanted to scream, "GO FUCK YOUR-SELVES!" It had nothing to do with the money. It was the indignity of squeezing blood out of a turnip that was nowhere to be found.

Thank God I had that email of empathy. My tears were tears of joy even if I was SAD and my BLUE became more of a LAVENDAR shade of pale…all thanks to Adriana's email.

Who Killed Kenny?

Jim was so polite. He would always send a text message to ask if he could call. I mean, who does that but a guy who truly doesn't want to impose. He was everything that was alive in a blue world. Blue car, blue jeans, blue shirt, blue sweaters, and blue suede shoes….it was his calling card and I liked it. At times I missed the texts but fortunately he'd then make the call and I'd know it was him from caller ID.

"Hi Jim, what's up?"

"I just thought I'd give you a heads up. Maggie May (that was Jim and Adriana's cute boxer who I was set to watch as they went off to New York) has come down with kennel cough."

"Sorry to hear that Jim."

"Yeah, we thought it best to leave her with Adriana's sister. Her dog died last year, and we don't want your dog, Sydney, to be exposed to Maggie's cough."

"I understand. No problem. Frankly, it's probably good for your sister-in-law to have Maggie around. It's tough to lose a dog…they really do become family."

We were definitely dog lovers. I had watched Maggie May a number of times and they had watched my Sydney. Our canines loved being around each other and their relationship strengthened the bond between their human beings.

"Yeah, Adriana and I came to that same conclusion. And of course, we would hate for Syd to get Maggie's cough." Jim was thoughtful and cautious when it came to a canine's health whether it was his or someone else's.

"Jim, did I mention when we had dinner the other night about my neighbor Kenny? I could never remember anymore what stories I shared. I suppose that came with age or perhaps because I was quite the Abe Lincoln of telling a yarn or two. It's said that Lincoln could disarm anyone, even those who didn't like him by sharing one of his anecdotal comical stories that were a bit poignant and definitely timely during the day in which the man lived. I loved telling stories and had plenty of them having lived in my world of color that comes with working at the Peacock Network of television.

"No…what about Kenny."

"He lost his little dog Angel, who at times could be downright mean. She was always nipping Syd who had a good 60 lbs. on her. I rarely dared to pet Angel, concerned she'd bite me, but Kenny loved his Angel and walked that dog three to four times a day. In doing so, he protected the block from intruders that had evil intentions and maybe fulfilled his obsessive curiosity. He knew everyone and their story and everyone on the block knew Kenny. In today's world, that's amazing considering most people don't even know the name of their neighbor be they to the right or left of their abode. Anyway, my former paramour - you remember, Myki? The designer who had quite the rack?"

Jim chuckled, "Yeah, who could forget Myki."

"I know…well on a day long ago during Spring she backed out of the driveway so recklessly that she almost hit Kenny and his Angel. After that happened, I couldn't help but ask her each time she pulled out of the driveway if she had killed Kenny yet?"

Jim inquired immediately with a smile in his voice, "Like Kenny in *South Park?*"

"Yep, like Kenny in *South Park,* who Stan, Kyle and Cartman kept killing over and over."

"Speaking of Myki…how's she doing?"

"Okay. She loves Florida. It suits her and her son, John Paul well. With his autism, he's better off in a small community filled with seniors where he can walk down the street without someone taunting him. You know, Myki wanted me to move with her down to the sunshine state, but I couldn't leave with Matt in the way that he was. Family first, love affairs second, sort of like how it used to be…country first, party second."

That actually got both of us laughing over our cellular divide. "So, how long's it been since you two lovers talked?"

"Uh…actually just a few days ago. I called Myki to tell her that I'd never have to worry about killing Kenny anymore."

"Why'd you tell her that?"

"Kenny suffered a fatal heart attack last week."

"Oh, sorry to hear that. So, who's going to watch Angel?" Jim sounded genuinely concerned and I could imagine him coming to the rescue but that wasn't necessary.

"No need to worry about that. Angel passed over that rainbow three weeks ago. It seemed that when Angel went, Kenny decided he'd had enough. All the twinkle in his eyes were gone, so was the smile he had for everyone including Syd. He seemed so forlorn when he made his walks all alone."

"That's so sad; it's a loss, no two ways about it, when our four-legged friends go, it hurts."

"Yep, that's why I've always said - DOG is an anagram for something so much greater."

When I got off the phone with Jim, I couldn't help but wonder if maybe that little bitch of a dog, the man's best friend, decided to go to the other side to prepare the way for Kenny. Isn't that what angels always do for those they love and protect? If so, then I've just shared a tale of bliss courtesy of a soul that wagged a shiny tail that offered a shade of pale filled with glorious light to offset the dancing shadows on the wall of that stygian passage we don't know but call the hereafter.

How's That Thirty Minute Chocolate Cake Comin'?

It was supposed to be only three months…okay, maybe six months. Not being naive, I figured more like a year. I had the notion of selling the house and heading WEST to the Land of the Sun when I got the call.

"Dad, can your grandson and I come live with you?"

"You're moving back to Chicago?"

"Yeah, I'm transferring from the Olive Garden in Rockford back to the one in Downers. I think I'll have greater opportunities to move up."

It was my youngest, technically my third youngest, but since the son had passed, by default she became the baby. The only thing she seemed to share with the older girls was their brother.

Two widowers, in their pursuit of romance while still relatively young did their best to blend but there was always a bit of *simple sister* imposed on the stepsister. Fortunately, the brother didn't buy into any of the half or step-blood-shit. To him they were simply sisters

She was only 3 when I came along, thus the DAD nomenclature with the best of intentions. But let's not forget that the road to hell was/is often paved with the best of intentions. Thus, began our relationship which was like I said, "Okay" - POUND #FarFromGreat.

The three or was it six months turned to years. And I didn't care. I saw reasons, I saw signs, that somebody somewhere had to throw the *youngest* one a lifeline so she could turn her life around. She and her brother had found themselves betting their lives on the trifecta of suicide, heroin addiction and mental health that often flushed them down that rabbit hole of *where the hell am I?* She made it out, he didn't.

Her son was growing up. The father had succumbed to suicide and left them to struggle on their own. Life was a BITCH and hardly a piece of cake for *simple sister* and sometimes her SON rebelled against his Mother. But with a bit of help, from a friend she deigned to call Grandpa, the son turned into a man the way water turned into wine for another SON following his Mother's directive.

What I enjoyed the most about this challenge was getting to know *simple sister*. There were times when we talked, just the two of us. Usually it occurred when *simple sister* came home from her work as a line chef.

Simple sister had found a passion, FOOD, and the power of that GLORIOUS FOOD. That passion helped her control the other cravings that at times nagged at her. But she was now into being a Mother having lost that privilege twice. Three strikes and she'd be out. It was now FOOD, GLORIOUS FOOD and the redeeming power that a nutritious diet brings to the body and the soul. Creativity in the world of FOOD was/is amazingly encouraged unlike some crafts where one must play it close to the vest. In a kitchen, your heart's desire might be the next big item on a menu.

Simple sister sat down across from me on the couch after she had grabbed a glass of Cabernet. I nodded, waiting. And then the stories flowed.

But the one I enjoyed listening to the most was the tale about the executive chef telling *simple sister* that someone had fucked up. "An important party will be coming into the restaurant for a birthday party and the day shift failed to bake a chocolate cake as ordered on the reservation ticket. I figured you can knock out a cake in thirty-minutes, seeing as how you've been a baker."

"Hmm, a chocolate cake like we make Chef, takes more like 50 minutes."

"Nope, all I can give you is thirty."

"Okay, but where do you really want me Chef… in the back baking or holding the line?" *Simple sister* pointed out to the Chef and to me in her telling of the story, that there were a ton of LINE orders due and that stress can be mind-fucking.

Chef elected to keep *simple sister* in the trenches directing the effort to meet the DEMAND while he went back. How much problem could a simple chocolate cake be?

That's when *simple sister* took a long draw on her Cabernet, smiled and said, "The VIP party came into the restaurant as predicted and I was told by the manager to handle their order personally. I slowed things down just a tad. Chef couldn't have had more than about four minutes before they entered. By seven minutes, their orders were in. Someone should have told the wait staff to slow it down a bit or offer more free drinks in light of the 'birthday' celebration for the wife of a senior executive of the restaurant consortium that owns us. Perhaps everyone was doing a bit of suck-up."

Simple sister sipped her wine. "Did I tell you there are eight in the Chicago area?"

"No. That many?"

"Anyway, I grabbed an assistant and we had their orders out in 9 minutes." She looked at me for approval. Since I didn't know whether that was good or not, I maintained my silence.

She continued, "I knew that half of Chef's 30 minutes had expired. My new DRAMA has become…will he make it in-time or will Chef be fuckin' CHOPPED?"

Maybe it was hearing her say the word, '*fuckin*', but whatever it was we bust out laughing. We were fans of CHOPPED. The laughter was infectious. *Simple sister* had more to tell. "So, I said in a very loud voice, that everyone in the kitchen could hear," she winked, "you know me, 'Hey Chef, how's that thirty-minute chocolate cake comin'?'"

"You didn't!"

"I did!" She was ebullient in her humorous shade of pale.

It's easy to crackle with insane laughter if you know all the players. Having met the Executive Chef, I could see steam coming out of his ears upon hearing *simple sister's* query.

Don't let anyone fool you, there is nothing easy about making a fabulous chocolate cake…here's a tip if you want the cake moist and dreamy, roll-in a bit of mayonnaise. You'll never go back to a chocolate cake that doesn't have that white shade of pale in its mix.

Those fireside chats late at night were for me pure treasure. Maybe not only my son was where he was supposed to be… maybe *simple sister* was where she needed to be.

We both had to deal with Mr. BLUE. That never changes when you lose the bliss of loving someone but if you can laugh about the antics of your beloved while celebrating the joy of their LIFE, that's vital, a vitality that's even more so with LOVE because without IT, LIFE's unbearable.

Sometimes on days when I'm really BLUE, I recount what I just shared with you.

"Hey Chef, how's that thirty-minute chocolate cake comin'?"

It helps my BLUE variate with a mixture of red and white smiley emoji shades of pale that produce an aura of LAVENDAR filled with HOPE. That's a destination unknown to man but I wanted to go there because my boy never made it home to die.

My only relief was visualizing a sea so blue filled with the laughter, smiles, uproariously comical eyes, of *simple sister* who was THISCLOSE to her brother that I knew he'd bust a gut of joy with US when he heard his sibling cry:

"Hey Chef, how's that thirty-minute chocolate cake comin'?"

I got BLISS from a girl who was anything but a *simple sister*. She was a GODSEND that helped me fix the hole in my heart.

There's Blood Everywhere

As it turned out on our arrival in Cleveland, we wound up in an apartment complex in suburban Parma Heights, which might sound a bit fancy but far from it. It was strictly blue collar. The moving van screwed up some of our furniture but since we weren't paying them for the move commissioned by NBC, they were lackadaisical regarding our complaints. It took almost 9 months to get a table they scratched badly repaired. There were boxes of stuff that somehow magically disappeared between Milwaukee and Cleveland and the moving guy didn't have a clue as to what happened. It was frustrating and perhaps an omen of what was to come.

A month after we moved in, we spent a Saturday afternoon checking out the Zoo with our daughter Renee. She was now walking and even though it was an overcast day with a touch of rain, it had been fun to watch the baby's reactions to the attractions. Upon entering the driveway, we spotted a large police van and two squad cars with flashing lights spilling onto the brick exterior of the complex and reflecting off the pools of rain on the driveway. Upon entering our building, we could see cops with clipboards interviewing neighbors, many that we still had yet to meet. We walked to our apartment at the end of the hallway. We couldn't help but see cops entering and exiting the door of the apartment across from ours. One of the cops left the door open enough to reveal blood-splattered walls. Furniture had been toppled over. The large mirror above the fireplace was shattered and glass shards appeared everywhere; bits and pieces on the chairs not knocked over, on the coffee table as well as the shag carpet. There was blood everywhere. It was a mess. My wife and I quickly scrambled to our apartment and ushered our little girl in. A cop approached us before we could close the door and said, "If you don't mind, I need to ask you a few questions?"

I can't remember which one of us posed the query, but it was inevitable. "What happened?"

The cop raised an eyebrow perhaps wondering why we had missed the obvious. "Your neighbors, the Clancy's suffered mortal gunshot wounds. We're trying to discover any detail that might aid in our investigation. Ma'am, did you happen to know them?"

"Nah, we're new." With a razor's edge to her voice she asked, "Are we safe here?"

The cop ignored the question and pressed on. "What about you sir?"

"Like my wife said…we just moved in about 3 weeks ago. As a matter of fact, we have yet to meet any of our neighbors. May I ask, was this a burglary? What's going on?"

"That's what we're trying to find out sir. As to Parma Heights, it's relatively safe, the crime rate is low."

"Two people shot dead hardly sounds safe. That's it! That's all you're going to tell us. My wife is here with our baby during the day. Do we need to worry?"

The cop continued to jot something on his clipboard. He then looked up at the couple in front of him, both with furrowed brows of concern. "I get it. My wife and I just had a baby girl as well. I'll recommend in my report that patrols check on this building."

From the bedroom we could hear a tiny voice, "Mommy… mommy!" My wife thanked the officer and then left us at the door to attend to our little one.

"From what I could see, it doesn't look like a break in. Sir, did you ever overhear them fighting?"

I didn't want to answer but I had often heard the couple's incessant screaming at one another. It was so boisterous that you would have to have been stone deaf not to notice. I caught the officer in the eye and nodded affirmatively.

"That's what I was afraid of sir; I think the enemy was within that apartment."

"Suicide?"

"Murder - suicide. Perhaps that might ease your wife's concern that it wasn't an intruder – but that's not official and," the cop winked at me, "you didn't hear that from me. Is there anything else you can add?"

I didn't know what else to say. We couldn't comment about what happened that day – fortunately we were gone when the slaughter occurred. "No, sorry."

The cop nodded. "Ok, thanks. Try to have a pleasant evening."

I think had we heard the gunshot explosions it might have been worse. We had never witnessed anything like that, and I'm sure the sound would have gotten stuck deep in the cobwebs of our psyche. We were both shaken and feeling a bit isolated; home wasn't a quick ninety-minutes of driving to Chicago as it had been when we were residents of Milwaukee. We were now a good 500 plus miles away from our family and friends in the Windy City. I had a job to go to with plenty of people to mingle with. My wife had a baby and little fraternization in her world with neighbors she didn't know and now would be afraid to meet. It wasn't long before isolation had a vice-like grip that sent my wife into a spiral of depression and me wondering what I could do to help.

Publicist Bob Knoll, a co-worker was also a gypsy like me moving from one town to another to climb that ladder of success. Frankly he was the publicity department since it only had one publicist in it – him. He worked under the auspices of Greg Stehlin, the Promotion Director. For a young guy, Knoll seemed to know everyone in the press in Cleveland and had great connections with the theater world throughout the state of Ohio. He and his wife hailed from Columbus, Ohio, about 150 miles to the south of Cleveland, not quite as far from home as we were from Chicago, but nevertheless they too felt a bit alone in a new city. Bob started a week or so ahead of me, so we were the newbies.

As men often do when they don't know how to handle the emotional needs of their significant others, they work as co-conspirators to suggest that the wives meet and find solace in one another since they're both women who understand why women are so erratic at times…spoken like a man who hadn't a clue. In retrospect it was stupid of us to think what might work for canines would also work for grown women.

The date was a disaster. Bob's wife claimed that mine threatened to attack her and that she had a foul mean-spirited temper. As to my wife's take on the *play date,* she had nothing nice to say about Ms. Knoll. She found her combative and a rube that insulted effortlessly whenever she opened her mouth. It was an embarrassment for all and a lesson for Bob and me that maybe - maybe indeed - men were from Mars and women were from Venus.

My wife was lost in a world of shadows and depression. Although we had only been in Cleveland a little over 60 days, she was adamant that she and the baby fly home to Chicago as soon as possible. The first trip home lasted 5 days. The next trip was 8 days and the next trip after that was 14 days. The time between excursions to Chicago grew shorter. The only way we could afford the flights was by ringing them up on a credit card and going deeper into debt. We already were dealing with college loans and although the salary was a nice bump up from Milwaukee, it wasn't enough to keep up with the incessant need to return to the Windy City. When Thanksgiving rolled around and we had been in Cleveland for about 9 months, we drove to Chicago but on the return trip to Cleveland I drove back alone.

"I might as well stay in Chicago for Christmas and the New Year. There's no point in the baby and me going back just to return a few weeks later." It didn't matter how much I protested about the unity of the family; a decision had been made and even my in-laws found it wise. I wound up driving back to Ohio alone.

Rather than return to an empty apartment in Parma Heights, I found myself putting in extra hours and working late. Station image campaigns and locally produced program promotions had yet to be executed because news priorities trumped both our time and facilities.

One of the local shows featured an immensely popular Cleveland Press columnist by the name of Dick Feagler. Feagler was on a par with Chicago's star columnist, Mike Royko, who wrote for the Sun-Times and later the Tribune. New York had its Pulitzer Prize winning Jimmy Breslin. Newspaper columnists like Feagler, Royko and Breslin were celebrities in their towns. They were not only widely read, but also feared by politicians who found themselves raked over the coals charred by commentary filled with irony and sardonic wit.

Since WKYC-TV3 was the only NBC O&O - owned & operated - television station that the Directors Guild of America did not have a contract with, I was free to direct the crew and the production from any studio or on location if the script called for it. I would eventually join the DGA but that would be years later.

I found myself assigned to produce and direct a series of promotional spots with Feagler. However, Feagler proved to be a bit elusive since he not only wrote six columns a week, hosted his weekly KYC TV program, recorded daily a five-minute segment for a news radio outlet and served as an emcee for numerous charitable events in addition to being in demand as a paid key-note speaker. Feagler was raking it in and although his contract demanded a promotional blitz for his show, the date and time for doing that was at his convenience. But eventually he had to meet the commitment and I found myself assigned to a studio session set for 7:30 p.m. – some 12 days before Christmas. There was no point in going home to an empty apartment after finishing my regular work in the office on that day, so I decided to have dinner at Bishop's Buffet, an affordable cafeteria in downtown Cleveland only a mere block-and-a-half away from WKYC.

The streets of Cleveland were decked with boughs of holly, decorative holiday lights and striped candy canes that would have made Ralphie Parker in the film classic, "A Christmas Story," proud. One of the retail shops near Bishop's Buffet had an outside speaker that trumpeted Christmas carols making the streets merry as falling snowflakes formed a winter won-derland. Outside of Bishop's, an elderly bag lady with skin as craggy as America's badlands topped with a Slavic babushka over a thatch of disheveled sandy brown hair and coal like eyes held a cardboard box top with words scrawled in black marker that read, "Hungry – Help?" When the notes of Franz Xaver Gruber's Silent Night wafted into the air, I was moved by the androgynous ghost of Christmas Past; I desperately wanted to do something as pedestrians bypassed the old poor woman with nary a second thought about her plight.

I checked my right pocket and fondled four quarters that I always kept on hand to guarantee that I had the necessary bus fare to get back to Parma Heights. ATM's were not available then nor were any of the banks open, so whatever action I took had to be measured; I suddenly found myself starving since I hadn't had lunch. It was only after I peered through the large pane of windows to my right to get a gander at Bishop's menu prices and surveyed my wallet to find five George Washington's, enough for dinners with drinks, that I felt confident to proceed.

"Miss, I mean Ma'am…ahhhh… If you will come with me," I said gently, "I will buy you something to eat." The bag lady gave me a quizzical look with an arched eyebrow that quivered like Elvis upper lip before replying in a boozy breath, "Just give me the money and I will buy my own damn dinner." I protested. I was worried that she might buy a pint of Ripple. She obviously didn't approve of my way of thinking because the next thing I was faced with was a torrent of expletives, "SHIT! What the fuck are we waiting for – let's go young man? I like Bishop's, that's why I beat off that sly silvered bitch trying to grab my corner." I was momentarily mortified by her toothless flash of a smile that made me wonder if she enjoyed shocking me.

That exchange should have been a huge red flag but I was overwhelmed by the spirit of Christmas and my duty to help my fellow man – in this case – fellow woman. We entered the cafeteria as an odd couple from different castes that drew a number of looks from patrons having their meatloaf with mashed potatoes and corn or roast turkey with cranberry and green bean dinners. The two specials included a choice of a non-alcoholic beverage. At slightly less than five dollars I knew I had both meals covered. I took the meat loaf and she chose the turkey and it all seemed fine until my new-found-friend addressed the help.

"C'mon – put more fuckin' gravy on that dried up bird… hey bitch, I expect more than a smidge of cranberry with those icky green beans." The manager just happened to bring in a tray of steaming turkey when he heard the outburst of my new kimo-sabe. "Knock off that kind of language if you want to eat here ma'am." He then locked his eyes onto mine, "And sir, don't bring street urchins in here; you ought to know better than that."

I could see that bag lady was about to erupt and so I grabbed her arm and pulled her close enough to whisper, "Don't say another fuckin' word or I'm not buying you dinner!" She cast me a look that would have withered a boutonniere had I been wearing one and hissed like a cat about to claw the eyes of a dog. "Fine, but I want a piece of pie – preferably a cream pie." And with the hand dexterity of a magician she somehow slipped a slice of coconut cream next to that turkey plate and cup of java without so much as a clink of a sound.

I was too embarrassed to protest. I knew I didn't have enough to cover the pie. Instead, I left my platter of food on the cafeteria tray runner and paid for hers, eager to get away. The cashier shifted her head and eyes onto that lonesome tray and said, "You know, you shouldn't do that." I nodded and said, "You're right but I haven't enough to cover it all since she grabbed the pie." The manager noticed as well and said, "I want you to leave sir. Bishop's has no place for freeloaders." To my surprise bag lady with tray in her hands agreed, "You know he's right young man." The manager received her affirmation with a look of triumph and demanded, "Hand me that tray and then get the hell out of here." The bag lady was already seated enjoying her hot meal by the time I left the cashier area. I never heard so much as a word of gratitude, but she did raise her coffee cup in a toast as I passed her on my way out into the cold.

When I returned to the studio, I was still hungry. I hit the vending machines just outside of the studio in a dreary poorly lit hallway and grabbed a cup of crappy coffee and some cheese crackers with peanut butter. The Technical Director, an avuncular easygoing kind of guy, smiled with a hint of disapproval, "Are you sure you want to put that crap into your system? Why didn't you go out and grab something edible?" When I revealed my night of horror at Bishop's he bellowed a guttural laugh while exclaiming, "That's a hell of a Ho-Ho-Ho for this time of year." I nodded and then we both got to work as Dick Feagler arrived, eager to record.

The TD must have shared my plight to Feagler because three days later in the Saturday, December 15, 1979 edition of the Cleveland Press, Dick made my tribulation the focus of his column with a black and white cartoon illustration and a headline that read, "Merry Christmas – hold the pie." Feagler changed it up a bit or perhaps the hearsay version he heard wasn't exactly as I shared it. However, Dick Feagler definitely had a Christmas column that was humorous and yet poignant as all Christmas columns should be or as Dick put it, "My friend now passes the woman with his eyes averted just like I do."

Our daughter at 19 months was old enough to appreciate the wonder of Santa Claus, that ubiquitous traveler who delighted in rewarding with presents all the children who had picked *Nice over Naughty*. The adults who loved her reveled in her joy and it made the holiday come alive. But it was also a time fraught with the strain of a family breaking apart. My wife did not want to return to Cleveland and had made it clear that she and the baby would continue to live at Grandma and Grandpa's home with no intent on returning to Ohio.

Living a broadcaster's life meant sacrifices that were understandable such as dealing with pitiful salaries in smaller markets, but now this decision made little sense to me since Cleveland was at that time a top ten market and the return on investment was finally paying off with decent compensation, excellent benefits and perhaps the most important factor - opportunity to advance as an executive with a major broadcasting entity such as NBC. At that time in late '79 and early '80, many women stayed home for the first or second year of an infant's life but with a college education and teaching experience, my wife could have returned to her career and we could have employed child care once the baby was walking and talking. Teaching school again would have provided an opportunity for the wife to meet other women her age and develop friendships and combat the loneliness that comes with living in a city other than home. We were still in America and even though Cleveland was saddled with the burning Cuyahoga River reputation, it had a good deal of culture to offer if you took the time to discover it.

The late 70's and early 80's in America was a time of economic struggle for many Americans with interest rates as high as 17% on a typical 30-year mortgage. That made the American dream of owning a home virtually impossible for many. Besides the exorbitant usury rates, people with good paying jobs faced bank demands for down payments as high as 20% of the purchase price.

It was a time when Americans had to wait in long lines just to purchase gas. People were shooting those who tried to jump the line. It was a time when America's eminence was challenged as diplomatic employees were taken hostage by the followers of Iran's supreme leader, Ayatollah Khomeini. It was a time when America was still reeling from the loss of the Vietnam War, the first conflict in U.S. history where the public as well as the press deemed it so. The aftermath of Vietnam and Watergate left many Americans convinced that their government would not or could not be forthright when it came to affairs of state.

Besides the energy crisis, America was plagued with inflation and high unemployment, so if you had a job with benefits and you were working, you were one of the lucky ones. Both of my siblings had also found themselves early in their marriages forced to travel.

In my sister's case, she was married to a man in the military and they not only traversed the U.S. from one coast to the next but also had a stint in Japan…talk about foreign – that was like night and day compared to living in another state.

My brother, a young doctor in search of a firm of experienced surgeons willing to train a promising associate had to move to Dayton, Ohio. That was the route he and his wife and three kids had to take for my brother to succeed in the career path he chose. My sister-in-law, an RN, wasn't necessarily happy about the move, but she understood that surgeons aren't born - they're made. America was on the move and the idea of living in the same neighborhood as you did when you were a kid or retiring from a job with a gold watch after lifelong service was becoming the exception. As a media pro still in my twenties, I had already worked for six broadcast companies, all owned by different corporations. Unlike my grandfather and father, who had long track records with the same employer, I could foresee that nowhere in my future would I be eligible for that iconic timepiece.

I felt desolate. I didn't know who to turn to because frankly I didn't want to admit that my wife took off and her parents made it all possible. Desolate turned into anger. One was lucky to have a good paying job during a recession and to have to give that up in the quest of a career was stupid. Why couldn't the wife see that? But my mind was made up; no matter how insipid this move to ditch Cleveland seemed, I had to figure out an exit and I knew I didn't want to lose my daughter. That sentence said it all.

I was more in love with that baby than I was with the wife. I was disappointed with the battles the wife waged with those we'd meet, like Ms. Knoll, but I was mainly upset about the battle we had when it came to the birth of that baby. I was not going to capitulate when it came to us being responsible. In my soul, we were responsible to that child in making sure she breathed the bounty of life – even if it was over a dead body – mine. That may seem harsh but that's what went down and the choice – my choice - divided us. Someone liked having their weekends free and easy without the burden that comes with raising a kid, but that wasn't on the menu as far as I was concerned. I made it clear that as a couple we would respect that seedling of new life, that we would nurture it to term and give it all the love it deserved. I will never find fault with the wife once that child arrived. Upon hearing the cry of that tot, the wife was baptized with the fire of unconditional love that never wavered. My distaste was over the battle we waged to have that kid upon its conception.

I actually got to hold the baby first, and I don't say that with any edge, but merely to note that her tiny finger grabbed for human touch and my little finger locked in step with the baby's rockabilly moves declaring, "I'm alive and kicking now that air has entered my lungs." Well maybe that would be the *thought* rather than the *quote*. Anyway, her filled lungs made for a powerful squeezebox that emoted a mighty wind of a cry.

And – NO – I wasn't about to walk away from my daughter even if it meant walking away from my career.

I had no idea what to say or what to do but I knew that I needed to come up with a credible reason why I had to return to shikaakwa the Indian word for garlic that Robert de La Salle pronounced Checagou in a memoir he wrote in 1679. So, I manufactured a story. But I kept it simple, "My mother-in-law is very ill. We need to return to Chicago because we now need to be care-givers for MOM." To my relief, no one questioned it. At least that's what I told myself - forever wondering if that were truly the case.

To my surprise, the General Manager, Neil Van Ells, who I had only met once upon my arrival called the GM in Chicago, Monte Newman, and asked if maybe they could help me out with a position. I was even more surprised when Newman called and discussed my resume, which Neil had obviously sent him a copy that he had gotten from my employee file. Monte had nothing in the way of promotion at NBC5 in Chicago, but he did have an engineering vacation relief engineer spot (about 6 months of work). "I see you've got some engineering experience with WGN. Would you like to work for us as an engineer?" What was there not to like? I'd get union wages and benefits that would probably mirror what I was making as an Assistant Promotion Director in Cleveland, so I said, "Yes sir."

And that was that. I had a good paying job for at least six months; that would give me time to figure things out, both professionally and personally. The folks at that Cleveland station couldn't have been nicer in helping me leave with grace and without a loss of face. Now when I think about it, I'm sure they all knew that I suffered a personal crisis of some kind that had little to do with my mother-in-law and more to do with the mother of my child. Who wants to tell anybody something that will burn you as weak or out-of-whack? But that's the battle I waged and for the first time in my life, I feared what tomorrow might bring. A little of me died in Cleveland but I wasn't going to give up hope about life. It was a lot more challenging than I expected but that's what made life unpredictable.

Even though Mr. Sun turned into a rainy day I wasn't going to let tomorrow get to me or the wife or the baby. I planned to stick by them. We were family and that's what families did no matter the adversity that life sometimes brings. But that didn't mean I hadn't been stuck in a nightmare waiting for the break of day, still holding on…albeit barely…because that's how I felt with the loneliness of living in a town that didn't match the excitement of sweet home Chicago.

As to having that child, the wife said her reasons why she didn't want the baby and I said mine as to why we had to have the child. I would not let her be until she capitulated and bended to my will as selfish as that sounded. When you're told children are not in your future and then one magically comes along, you just can't throw that chance away. So, now that we had that joy, I wasn't going to allow her to abscond my Pumpkin to a city far, far away even if it was my hometown.

On the day of the birth of our joy - when the mother held her flesh and blood - she never said it, but the truth was plain to see. She knew I was right. I knew I was right.

That little bundle of joy brought us bliss. There was no point in ever discussing the matter of friction ever again. I decided to let the sunshine in and bask in the glow of the greatest gift one could ever wish for as a father, the bliss of having a daughter as beautiful as my Pumpkin – my Renee, which means spiritually born again.

God bless the child!

Phone Call for Help

"They just won't talk to me. They listen to you; they listen to their father. Please talk to them. I don't want them shutting me out of their lives…I'm their mother for God's sake."

She had a point. Even though we were no longer together as man and wife, was no reason we couldn't treat each other with some affection as parents. The girls were wrong to do what they were doing to their mother. The fact that she was my EX didn't make me waver on that one.

I tried to talk to the daughters, but it didn't matter what I said.

The younger of the two sisters shared an email in which her mother basically chewed her out over her personal life. When they're adults, you really can't do that to them. I knew that. How did my EX miss the center of the storm she'd magically gave birth to by unnecessary meddling?

The other or oldest one shared a story. It seems Mom embarrassed that daughter by noting before a party of four, the faux pas, "Oh and don't ask…she's still not married."

As bad as that might have been, I wasn't sure those infractions deserved life-time banishment…not from your own flesh and blood.

I was told in no uncertain terms by both of my daughters that I should stay out of it.

And so, I did. But then one of the daughters made me a target. I was caught in the same quicksand as my EX - talk about uncomfortable and a bit Kafkaesque.

TWO parents – TWO daughters that now talk to ONLY ONE of their parents…and they think that's OKAY?

Actually, it's not! No one is perfect in life…maybe in death, but never in life. Perhaps for the daughters they enjoyed a bit of bliss and independence that a parent has to accept if they truly love their children.

The Book Owl

I met her on FACEBOOK. She was the QUEEN of a book club by the name of "WINE ABOUT BOOKS." Get it? Cute!

I asked her if her group would consider reading my book and allowing me to be there to listen to what I got right or maybe what I got wrong. I was a local author, no big deal. I had a book about to be released and genuine feedback would have been most appreciated.

"No, I don't think we could do that. But you're welcome to come and drink some wine with us. The book we're currently reading is *White Collar Girl*, by Renee Rosen. You've still got 13 days before we meet to read the book."

Her voice sounded inviting. I was hooked and said, "Okay."

She sent me a private message via Facebook with all the details.

I bought a copy of the book since the three copies that the Library had were already checked out.

White Collar Girl is a great tale about a woman who wants to be a journalist. She works at the Chicago Tribune during the 50's and finds that no one can picture her covering anything other than the social scene. But despite the freezing cold of a glass ceiling of ICE – shear ICE – the kind that kills you if it shatters and sends a shard your way, was a young woman willing to shed a bit of blood, sweat and tears in order to capture her dream to become a significant journalist.

I had a blast at the *WINE ABOUT BOOKS* book club. It was at a restaurant where we could order vino (of course) and what I would call TAPAS artistry that included the tastiness of a porcini pizza loaded with wild mushrooms.

The Queen of the Club had a ginger-auburn crown of hair that was absolutely stunning. She had delicate Danish features and was almost as tall as me but not quite. But her look, albeit sweet, was not why I was attracted to her. She had a sardonic wit. She was intelligent and she made it clear during our very first conversation that she was a 5-minute-kind-of-gal. Now if you don't know what that is, let me educate you. A 5-minute-kind-of- gal is a woman that will be very intense with you for an unspecified amount of time, usually no more than three to four weeks when you are then dumped so that she can move onto further boredom.

We were having dinner when she shared her *5-minute theory* with me. We were on our third date, so, you know the nasty was but a song away.

Maybe she wanted me to protest such nonsense or possibly to engage in a fight with her. It's an Old English dream to fight and then enjoy make-up sex. But my pride wouldn't let me reveal how I really felt about the woman with the Ginger-Auburn hair. I wanted more of this woman, but I wasn't going to give up my soul for her either. That may sound stupid but after you've had your heart stomped on a couple of times you have a tendency to smile a bit less. I really wasn't into playing games. Instead I poured us both another glass of RED (not sure if it was a CAB or a Pinot) and clinked glasses with a woman I really liked but was sure would soon be gone in a NY minute.

She then leaned into me for a kiss. We locked on as if we weren't going to let go. Maybe the third date was the charm. All

I know is that we couldn't wind up anywhere because she had grown kids and so did I. We were too old to do it in the car and a motel sounded too cheesy. Instead we went to hear a tribute band that could play *Stairway to Heaven* to a T. It was crowded and so we literally stood before a band with my arms encasing her as we heard the guitar licks created by a Jimmy Page wunderkind as she turned back to me and I kissed her over and over and over and over again and again.

I also liked the fact that she had such a fascination with the lifestyle of Medieval England where Yorkshire pudding was always part of the menu. The Ginger-Auburn hair woman loved to dress up in the clothing of the day. She had a great costume. She looked like the country wench who served men their quaffs of beer wearing of course a push up bra that made her already abundant rack even more abundant. I loved looking at her in that costume. It brought out the very best of her and me because her bosom was truly a sight to behold.

She then did something for me that was so sweet, so very sweet. On a day when I couldn't make it, she told the other Book Club participants that we would all be reading for the next month's meeting a book written by the colleague absent that evening. Yeah….my book. That was truly a gift. The sex was amazing that night. We found a classy place, the apartment above the theater where I served as a board member, where out of town actors about to be in one of our productions could stay. We grabbed it on the days when it was empty. That's where we made love again and again and again, slowly, intensely, and passionately.

We were into month five. I had introduced her to one of my grown children who had returned to live with me with her son.

I was sure that we had made a connection. Someday I might recover from that silly naïve way of thinking but I had gotten hooked into that Old English dream. I didn't want to sleep in the cold anymore. I loved having the warmth of her next to me even on nights when we didn't penetrate any membranes but merely held each other within our arms. But all of that promise went up in smoke when she said, "I think our 5-minutes is UP." I couldn't see any part of a soul when I looked into those aloof-blue-eyes. I must admit that the rest of my BOOK OWL appeared incredibly moist. But our 5-minutes were UP! I wasn't going to shatter that Old English dream because all dreams naturally dissolve when you wake up.

Now whenever I hear, "Stairway to Heaven," I think about that Ginger-Auburn lady who loved to dress up as a wench serving Pilsners in a forest that echoed with laughter. I can't help but remember that bliss with a bit of regret. I wished we had fulfilled my Old English dream of being with someone I adored for more than a mere 5-minute window. I suppose I was falling in love with her and that made a cynical man feel hopeful.

Every now and then I share a recommendation for a great book with the BOOK OWL via the cyber world. In the cyber world you don't have to worry about a 5-minute window. It's more like thirty seconds but I have no regrets but only fond memories of my 5-minute window with the BOOK OWL.

I'll never be able to figure out the BOOK OWL. I do know one thing without a doubt. She's quite the PROGRESSIVE. So was I but not quite as committed to the revolution as she was. That's okay. I'm richer in life because of the BOOK OWL and that blessing is as good as any Old English dream.

No Glinda – but a Witch for Sure!

I loved watching "The Wizard of OZ," with the old man. He had the deluxe Blue Ray DVD with all the special features. Glinda was a witch, but she was GOOD. The old man often would call her Belinda or even Brenda. I'm not sure why he had that confusion because papa was always spot on with his movie trivia - but hey, he was getting older and I noticed that from time to time he had a problem remembering names.

The old man not only loved film but the arts in general. He was a big supporter of SEASPAR, the 501c that made the park systems of Du Page County better for many kids and adults with disabilities. SEASPAR offered programs for those with disabilities that included trips to the cinema, theatrical plays, museums and zoos. They had an annual fund raiser at the TIVOLI Theater – a grand old theater in the style of 30's DECO – that featured a class act – a tribute band that was supposedly awesome.

At least that's what I heard but a DOG even with an exceptional vocabulary like mine has at times a problem with the nuances of Human Speak. Did you know that a DOG is capable of understanding some 2,000 words? Well, the gifted ones can and if I say so myself, and I do, I run in that pack.

As a TV producer, my Master had directed a few documentaries employing his only son Matt as a sound tech. Both of them loved NPR, which they had on all the time in the car. I guess I was lucky to be part of family that helped me to be very, very smart for a canine.

I'm aware of the details regarding SEASPAR because every night I sat next to the old man on the couch while he reviewed social media posts and local upcoming events on his laptop. It seems there was a younger woman, twenty years his junior who had been flirting with him on FB. It all seemed innocent enough because she lived in Rockton, about 100 miles away. Rockton was next to Rockford where the old man had started in TV, where his kids Matt and Melissa, had as young adults lived with his ex-wife at one time and where their grandparents and some of their aunts and uncles called home. It's where Melissa continued to live, but on her own with her fiancé Ryan.

Based on what I was able to ascertain, Brenda was a successful artist and author of children's books. She claimed to have created numerous stories and the accompanying artwork. She also proudly announced that she had a deal with a major drug store chain willing to distribute and sell her work nationwide.

I was surprised that my guy continued to flirt back on FACE-BOOK (FB), but it had been a long time since he had a girlfriend. The fact that this Brenda babe knew a few of the old man's professional colleagues probably convinced him to dismiss any fear that she was a troll trying to entice an older guy for his wallet.

There was no doubt in my DOG mind that the old man found Brenda attractive. He shared with his buddy Phil that his newfound playmate's photos on FB featured her with "*big, big boobys*" - whatever those were and was quite the "*looker*" – whatever that meant. I always had a problem with slang but in time I figured it out.

I don't think my old man ever expected the two of them getting together. They lived miles apart. But there was that extra

SEASPAR ticket he had bought for Matt who was sidelined to a hospital stay with a broken leg in traction due to a nasty motorcycle accident. The old man shared the news of Matt's wipeout via FB messenger with Brenda and asked if she'd accompany him to the show? The FB messages somehow lead to phone calls and the two of them would yak, yak, yak for hours about everything under the sun including how they dealt with all the nut jobs on Facebook that drank too much Kool-Aid in their inanity to worship some orange guy that tweeted out stupid shit every morning when he took a 3 a.m. dump. I could relate since I often needed to go out about that time to take a whiz.

When they did talk, it was about the upcoming concert; the old man promised Brenda that they'd have a great time listening to a band by the name of Tributosaurus known for its remarkable ability to cover to a "T" (whatever that meant) the music of another band called JOURNEY. It was a bit complicated for me to get but I could tell from the "ooh's" and "ah's" emanating from the old man's cell phone which I heard via my extraordinary aural powers that Brenda was excited as well. The old man promised to pick up the cost of a nice dinner if she'd come to Downers Grove. She agreed. She asked my papa to send information regarding hotels near-by, since she didn't think it would be a good idea for her to try and drive all the way back to Rockton, about 100 miles away, following the show.

The old man insisted that he was merely looking for companionship and didn't want the ticket to go to waste. He made it clear he didn't expect anything else. I wasn't exactly sure what "anything else" referred to – another case of jargon beyond a DOG's initial grasp. To his credit, when ages were revealed, papa indicated that he was old enough to be Brenda's father – and allowed her an opportunity to back out.

"I don't care," she said. "My father's your age but based on your Facebook photos which I'll assume our recent, I'd say you look a good ten to fifteen years younger. Has anyone ever told you that?" The old man's eyes filled with the light of utmost happiness. I knew he knew the answer to that question because Matt often told his father how young he looked compared to his actual age.

On the day of the concert, I heard another call. "Brenda, you haven't reserved a room?" The old man sounded concerned and maybe a bit anxious.

I could hear Brenda through the phone give her explanation as to why she hadn't booked a motel reservation. "It's not a problem, if necessary, I can always stay at my mom's as long as I keep myself to a couple of wines – I'll be fine." She went on to note that her mother lived a mere 8 miles away in the nearby suburb of Wheaton.

"Okay, but if you need to stay here, I can stay at my buddy's place for the evening. I'll have to leave my dog SYD at the house, but she's a sweetheart."

Wow! Was he dropping all of that responsibility on me? I frankly found it a bit too much even for a very, very smart DOG. As it turned out, Brenda stopped at the house before the concert to meet me…at least that's what she said when she walked in. "Oh, and this must by SYD or is it Sydney?"

The old man always like to punk me when it came to my name, so I wasn't shocked when he said, "Yes, that's Syd Vicious – in the flesh." Fortunately, Brenda realized the joke and smiled; she pet me over and over exclaiming, "SYD's way too nice for that and way too beautiful." I must say at that moment Brenda had me.

I also must say that she looked a lot like Glinda in OZ with those beautiful golden tresses and my, my - she rocked quite a figure. Then the two of them were off to a swanky restaurant for dinner prior to attending the concert.

They didn't return for several hours. After getting back to the house they drank several glasses of Cabernet Sauvignon and thought nothing of ignoring me while they went on and on about the music of Journey and how well the tribute band had performed. What bothered me was how their focus shifted from talking to touching as they intertwined their fingers like a *slow dance*, or do I mean *slow trance?*

Then the old man announced his desire to depart from the premises.

"Brenda, it's late. I'd better head over to my buddy's place. I've got a key, but I don't want to enter his place after midnight and wake him up. By the way, the bedroom made up and ready to go for you to use is right over there." He pointed and she nodded as he continued. "I'll be back in the morning and maybe we can catch breakfast before you hit the road. Oh, don't be surprised if SYD joins you in bed at some point."

Really? Oh c'mon, this bitch (me) had no intention of jumping into bed with that Brenda- Bitch!

But then Brenda did an eye roll and said rather seductively to papa, "But I don't want you to go. Can't you stay a bit longer? I haven't been out in a long time. After the divorce I just didn't feel like getting back into the dating game. I still find this all a bit amazing – how we met on Facebook – who saw that coming? Anyway, I'm enjoying the moment, aren't you?"

"Absolutely." The old man snuggled even closer to the Bitch and smiled, "Sure, I can stay if you want. I don't have to work tomorrow, so why not? More wine?"

WHAT? I was pissed! I'm the only bitch that the old man needed in his life. He was falling for Brenda the troll with the big chest. I have quite the core and I could appreciate how alluring that could be. I thought she was taking advantage of a man a bit fragile from his divorce, concerned about his son's injury and maybe missing the allure of a sexy female.

After another sip of their wine, their lips locked as they kissed over and over and over and over and over. I wound up having to sleep on the couch that night as she moved into the master bedroom with the old man. Wow, that was *our* bed. Oh-that did it! Brenda the BITCH had to go. I wasn't sharing or giving up my spot of snuggling next to my man without a fight.

When morning came, papa flashed a grin that reminded me of one of those old Buick cars with the huge grill of chrome reflecting teeth that we often spotted at a summer Friday night car show. I had to admit it if only to myself, the old man did have a twinkle in his eye, which I had not seen for some time. I reluctantly accepted that the old man *got laid* – a phrase I did understand.

The façade of being a successful author/illustrator disappeared the morning after as she shared with the old man her financial struggles and the legal issues she faced. It seems that the gifted successful children's author was plagued with a deadbeat dad while she raised a teenage son and two daughters. Brenda was also tied up in some kind of legal battle with the drugstore chain regarding her books. She went from being a smooth operator to a sniffling weeping soul in my canine opinion.

All of those tears touched the old man's heart. It started out innocently enough with her declaration that she didn't have the funds to get her blood pressure medication and could possibly die. "What am I going to do?"

Papa, being the-nice-guy that he was, insisted that he would come to the aid of his damsel in distress. Brenda feigned a response that even I found insincere. "Oh, but I couldn't ask you to do that." But papa persisted and then she insisted that she would pay him back the $300 for the prescriptions. That's when she pulled him close and sealed the deal with a wet kiss. It was obvious to even a DOG that she was using her charms to extract money from her newly found ATM.

After that exchange, we made several trips to Brenda's place in Rockton. I hated that damn ride and I hated the fact that she had cats and I hated that I had to sleep on the floor rather than in a bed. I tried once to jump up on the bed they shared only to be rejected by both of them because they were too busy cavorting. The indignity of that rebuff was mind boggling.

The old man may have been twenty years older, but it was Brenda who was plagued with health issues. She was like a car that looked great on the outside but under the hood was a disaster. The old man continued to help her pay for all the different medications she required, and they weren't cheap.

She had the old man "wrapped around her finger," an expression I often heard on a soap opera that papa watched with regularity. I got the nuance of that one.

The old man's friends, Phil and Chuck, were amazed that their longtime amigo was dating someone two decades younger. They wanted "details," but the old man did little more than give them a smile. However, he did accept their "high fives," which was another phrase I had never heard before but when I saw the move, the meaning was obvious.

As a DOG, I have not only a great nose for detecting a scent, but I am also able to discern anxiety and moods. And then I witnessed the biggest hit. After some steamy sex, Brenda the foxy 35-year-old purveyor of children's books that preached the importance of virtue and righteousness asked if papa could please pay her $1,000 rental house fee that was due in ten days. Brenda claimed she didn't have the money and was desperate. She promised when she got her $5600 tax refund, which she shared convincingly by displaying her prepared tax return as proof – that she would promptly pay him back the loan.

I saw the old man fall for it. He gave her a check. Brenda even signed what she described as a promissory note. But despite being a DOG, I could see what the old man failed to see because he was bewitched and captivated with her charming chest. Unfortunately, he was being had. In all the old man gave Brenda The Troll some $1700 in less than the fast of forty-days Jesus endured in the wilderness. But when she asked for his credit card number so she could put her utilities on it, a light went on in his head. He withdrew and got off the phone with her abruptly after shouting a vociferous, "NO!"

Fortunately for the old man, his brother took him on a road trip to Mount Rushmore in South Dakota. It was good for him to get away from that Bitch. It gave him a bit of time to reflect on a relationship in which one gave and the other took and took and took. However, his absence was not good for me. I had to reside with his oldest daughter who had way too many rules.

Upon his return, Brenda invited us to Rockton. She did cook for us. It was supposed to be a three-day Friday through Sunday night visit. The beef stew she made was delicious and she even made sure I got a bowlful.

To papa's credit, he denied her incessant demand for more money. "Listen Brenda. I don't think it's healthy for our relationship that you keep asking me to prop you up. I hear you on the phone with your clients. You're charging big bucks for a drawing. Where's all that money going?"

Brenda frowned. She then began to tear up which quickly turned into a crying jag. In the middle of her sobs she blurted out, "If you really loved me, you'd take care of me without making it an issue. I take care of your needs and I'm looking forward to doing it again tonight." He retorted, "I have taken care of you and your demand for more and more money doesn't sit well with me. Frankly I can't help but think you're using me and plying me with sex as the carrot to get me to pay for it… that's not a loving relationship and you know that."

Wow! That didn't sit well with her and then all hell broke loose. I ran for cover under the bed.

I got to hand it to the old man. After the war was over, he put my leash on and we walked out. Hallelujah! The spell of Brenda the Witch had been broken and we were no longer in OZ but instead clicking our heels home.

That night I snuggled up closely to the old man in our bed and in my head, I heard that song, "Ding Dong the Wicked Witch is dead!" Actually, she wasn't literally dead but once the old man turned on someone, he didn't turn back.

It was only much later, at least a good six months when the old man took me for a ride to the courthouse in Wheaton. He dressed me in my red and white Santa Claus coat because it was a bit chilly that December day. I was familiar with the building and the parking lot having gone there before when the old man had to deal with a traffic ticket. I was mystified as to why we made the trip because had there been a traffic infraction, I would definitely have heard papa bitch about it.

I wound up taking a nap in the back seat. I doubt if anyone noticed me because the garage where we parked was dark. I expected the old man to be gone and he was for a good 30 minutes. When papa returned, he had a smile on his face that looked just like that '53 Buick with the big metal grill. He patted me on the head and said, "SYD, we won baby. I even got a payment schedule. Brenda has to pay me back every cent she owes. Let's hit the dog park and celebrate."

While at the park, when I wasn't sniffing another dog's butt, I got to reflect on what had transpired over the last several months. Matt was back. He was healthy and that brought joy to his father. I loved Matt as well. He always made it a point to cook something for me when he prepared dinner. He loved to spice it up but was always sensitive to what I could and couldn't digest.

As to what the old man had been through, I never doubted that he truly cared about Brenda which based on what even this canine noticed meant little to her. I'm sure some would have labeled him an "old fool" but I remembered what Jay said in the *Men in Black* movie: "*It's better to have loved and lost than never to have loved at all.*" The old man and Matt loved that movie, so we caught it with regularity via something they referred to as, "on-demand." Life was good and bliss was all around us!

Shame on you Brenda – you're no GLINDA – but you are a WITCH – even a DOG knows better. I may be a bitch but that's only because I'm a female canine. What's your excuse BITCH with a capital B?

Yeah, you bet I felt bad for the old man. He deserved better, but don't we all?

Dial Tones

I tossed and turned, but with the help of my trusty dog by my side, I finally fell into a deep slumber filled with the sounds of dial tones. The tones weren't of the caliber one might hear when one picked up a phone or fired up a cell. They were the tiniest of tones, the kind you get when you actually punched a letter or number from a keypad. It was so pervasive that it had a stygian aura to it that I knew I would have to track down and figure out if I was ever going to R.I.P.

I sat up in the bed, which annoyed trusty dog who got up and did a wolf like twirl only to plop down on the edge of the bed making sure that contact between our warm bodies on this very cold, cold winter's night was verboten. To say that my Syd was a bit pissed at all my tossing and turning was an understatement.

I began to try and recognize the beeps. I grabbed my cell and began to punch keys that matched the tones I heard. In my musical lifetime I filled the air with chords of an Accordion playing *Lady of Spain* for my grand ma-ma before I transitioned to the flute and drums of my rock days and then musical stylings of a middle aged piano man having a midlife crisis, empowered me the wherewithal to recognize the notes of those tones and bang them out on my cell. I was sure there was a number I had to call. Otherwise, why was I hearing those tones, those fuckin' tones that drove me crazy. It was like a time bomb ticking down its clock or nails on a chalk board or whatever image you want to insert that truly makes you shiver inside your soul because it's just SO FUCKIN' annoying!

It was a very strange number. When I was sure I had gotten the pattern of dial tones right, I had what I assumed was an international number. I had a flight booked for Buenos Aires in the near future, a place I had always wanted to see where I could experience the music and pageantry of the tango, perhaps even gain insight to those moves from a lovely Latina. I was flying solo then and a lovely Latina did sound exciting. I hope that desire doesn't offend anyone.

But back to the call. I checked and double checked the pattern of the tones to discover that I had discovered a code of sorts that lead to a number that appeared long enough to be traveling long distance. And that's exactly what it was.

The call was outside of EARTH. How could that be? But I noticed that on the other end I didn't hear an accent or a language I recognized. As a matter of fact, I didn't hear a single word and yet I knew exactly what was being communicated.

"Good Day, how may we in peace help you?"

"I'm sorry. I don't understand. Who did I reach? Who are you?"

"It must be a shock - sir? But you can talk to anyone you want who ever lived? But you only get to pick one."

There was a moment of black as coal silence.

"Need I elaborate sir?"

"Then let it be my son."

"Name please…there are a lot of souls here."

"He goes by DJ Boraichee even though his first name is Matthew – Matt."

"Okay, I'm going to put you on hold and no matter how long it takes, don't disconnect because you only get this kind of a GO AROUND but once sir."

I would stay on hold till I died if that's what it took. I damn well wanted to make a connection. The last time we talked was on the day he left. It was more of a smile and what talk there was ensued from men sitting behind the wheels of their autos looking at one another out from the driver side windows of those vehicles.

The *quiet* disturbed me. It gave me too much time to reflect on my sins, the sins of the Father who let the SON down. I tried at first to convince myself that he was an adult and I wasn't culpable for what he did. But after a lot of sleepless nights you realize you never find peace until you come clean with your share of a disaster. When someone passes, in a good or bad way, everyone in his or her inner circle had some responsibility for how that life was lived.

I just didn't get it. I couldn't understand how Matt could be so cautious about what he inserted into the recipe for a dinner he was creating and yet so careless when it came to that which he injected into his blood. I knew I'd never want to be around such a mess. Why didn't he feel the same way?

And that's why we were so alike and yet so different. I wanted too much for him and frankly it wasn't up to me to do the "wanting." It was his life to find *success*. It's a shame I didn't get that maybe my vision of *success* wasn't necessarily Matthew's take on that elusive frame of mind we as a society deign to call *happiness*.

My cell came alive and I heard, "Hey dad! Is that you?"

"Yeah Matt…it's me buddy…your old man, the guy you fought with day and night and it's only now that I realize I didn't help you prepare for that sail to parts unknown. I was lost. I was friggin' lost!"

"No sweat dad. I wouldn't want to go back where you're at, although I miss you and mom and of course my sis, but, once you've experienced where I'm at, you'd never trade places with that kind of life again."

I could detect a smile, a lilt in his voice that I never heard during his stay on EARTH.

"How do you feel?"

"I feel at ease. I don't hurt. I'm not depressed. I don't have migraines. I don't have that look in the mirror like I did on EARTH of a loser. I wouldn't believe it exists but I'm living it so it must be so. And yes, we are very much alive with a sense of bliss that is so incredibly delicious that you are never ever hungry. The light here beams a shade of pale that is indescribably joyous."

"Wow…that sounds so, so, enticing! I am so overwhelmed. I'm thrilled for you and now I hurt a bit less, thanks to you son."

"Remember when I sang that ditty from Indian Guides? "Pals forever Dad…I love you!"

I recalled the moment in time. The sands were so white, the sea so blue and the skies so true to the color of his eyes at the Indiana Dunes Park when we recorded those messages for the upcoming Father's Day tribute video. Each dad got a version of "Pals forever Dad…I love you!" from their little Indian Guide.

"I'll never forget that one Matt."

"Well it's as true today as it was then. It's just space and time between us dad. There's no point in me trying to explain it. You'll get it as soon as you go through the tears of joy known by EARTH as death. Death is the beginning of life dad. I actually feel a bit sad for you."

"Sad. No, No. I'm here for a reason. I know most would laugh at that, but that's how I feel."

I could hear running through the line or was it the connection or whatever fantasy it was for me to have this call, the beat of one of his mixes. He had been a DJ.

"I can't tell you how pleased I am son with this call. It will help me realize my old English dream."

I could hear his laugh. It was so good to hear because he rarely laughed when he was going through withdrawal. The laugh was infectious; I joined in.

"What in heaven's name is that dad?" His voice smiled and before I could reply he said, "I might have expressed that on EARTH a bit differently."

"I'm sure you would. Praise the Lord, I now can die in peace."

"Not yet…no tears of joy for you just yet dad. Remember? You've got a reason for being there and I'll bet that maybe you don't realize the full extent of it yet, but, I know what you did for so many novices trying to get a foothold in an exciting endeavor. Even here, they all still love to talk about what they saw on TV in the land down under - get it? That's what we call it – as strange as those Aussies are…just kidding dad."

I couldn't help but chuckle. A weight had been lifted off my soul. I felt lighter, brighter, and wiser.

"How's Snickers?"

"Good question son, I need to check on your cat."

"Hey dad, they're telling me I've got to go, there's quite the line or the queue as you would say for this phone. Reminds me of when I'd call you from prison."

I laughed. He laughed. We laughed and laughed and laughed and laughed and laughed until I laughed so hard, I woke myself up. But I don't care what anyone says. To me that conversation was as REAL as REAL could be…and I had the proof. The cell was still aglow, and I saw the caller ID with all those digits.…

WAIT A MINUTE, I'm not about to reveal that. You'll have to find that one out for yourself.

What had been a pain in the ass, those incessant DIAL TONES burrowing into the recesses of my mind had undergone a chrysalis that converted an unforgettable memory into an unforgettable blessing.

Yes, yes, yes! That was quite the call. A perfect call as the drumpf might say.

I was blessed with bliss and what more can one ask of fatherhood than to live that old English dream where your son buries you? Maybe the bliss wasn't what it all was cracked up to be – at least not in this case but I'd take what God handed me and make the best of it…that's what Matt would have wanted his father to do and that was good enough for me.

Snickers

Snickers was a bi-color cat. In other words, she was a magpie, a black and white feline. She was good natured, much like Matt the love of her life.

Snickers was also known as a tuxedo cat which ranged from six pounds to twenty pounds. Snickers was a little over thirteen pounds. She had a lot of fur that stood up as if someone plugged her into an electric socket. That fluffy fur made her look even bigger. If she was a woman, we'd probably characterize her mane as that of a chick from Indiana with BIG HAIR. You know the type.

However, there was no way Snickers could have existed in the same house with my trusty dog SYD. SYD hates cats. She even hates little dogs that look like cats. That is the only negative quality I can truly attribute to SYD, a loveable easy going GONCZY – a Polish breed that possessed the incredible ability to sniff out a scent even at ten feet underground. The Police loved the breed for cadaver searches. That explained in part why SYD often pulled on her leash till she got over to a scent she picked up fifteen feet away. The other item we should also note is that SYD was as strong as a horse. That girl could yank you so hard that if you weren't careful, your arm was going to be pulled from its socket. If SYD went after Snickers, she might kill the cat or lose an eye scratched out of her head. Some cats don't take any shit from a dog no matter what. I wasn't sure which kind Snickers was and I didn't want to find out.

I made it clear when my adult son was forced to live with his father per a court order or sit in a cell, that we'd have to find another home for Snickers, his beloved cat. Matt had the acumen and the sensitivity to bond with an animal, be it a cat or a dog. He treated his pet like she was a sister or better yet, one of his progeny. Matt fought me on the suggestion, but I told him I didn't want SYD losing an eye, and that was enough for him to make the sacrifice. He had met SYD a number of times and really liked her. They got along great and a lot of that had to do with Matt's ability to ride on the same wave as the animals he loved. I think Matt could somehow find a way to inculcate himself into the souls of that dog and that cat. Unfortunately, they became mortal enemies since SYD would never willingly acquiesce her territorial claim as the one and only pet in the house.

I assured my son, "Snickers won't go to a kill shelter. I'll find Snickers a nice home, maybe one where you can visit her."

"You promise?"

"You have my word Matt."

I tried first to see if Matt's mom would take Snickers, but she claimed to have developed an allergy to cat hair. That seemed strange because when we were together, we had cats. I got a sense she wondered if I wondered how one gets an allergy later in life…but it was legitimate, and it does happen. I then posted on Nextdoor.com about our predicament and would someone be willing to take the cat for 3 to 6 months. Matt was confident he could be out of my house in that timeframe and then he'd take Snickers back. Eventually I did find someone to take Snickers who Matt approved of.

I was on NEXTDOOR.com posting something on behalf of a charity I worked for as a volunteer board member when I noticed I had a message from someone reacting to my post.

> *Hi Matt's dad, I saw your post about Community Adult Day care. I have just been praying during the last few days that God would direct me to some way that I can volunteer, especially with the elderly. I think maybe your post might be the nudge I was needing. Are you involved with this facility? Do you know if they need volunteers? My elderly mother died in December and now I have more free time and also an inclination to try to serve the elderly. BTW you might remember my name although we've never met. I am Snickers' new mom. I think about your son often. :) Ellen*

I remembered Ellen even if we'd never met. She answered my inquiry regarding Snickers and took the cat under the assumption it would be for a few months. She had a husband, kids and a cat and for the near future would be happy to take Snickers in and help us out. I had Matt follow up with her via cell and he brought Snickers over to her temporary new home where he met the new parents and ingratiated himself with the family. Matt wanted to make sure Snickers got to keep the name he had given his feline. My son also wanted to able to visit Snickers. Ellen was kind enough to say, "No problem, you'll always be welcome."

My impression at the time she took Snickers in and even after Matt died was pure bliss. This was a woman who understood the word empathy. When I spoke with her to tell her what happened to Matt and that I'd come and get the cat, she said,

"Of course if you want Snickers, she's yours, but I've got to tell you, my husband loves that cat and if you'd like us to take care of Snickers, we will." I felt the weight of an albatross removed from my back. "Wow. That sounds great! Yes. Please do. Thank you."

On that evening when I got Ellen's message, I replied as follows:

> *Hi Ellen - I'm the president of the Board of Directors of the charity you're inquiring about. I got involved with CADC because my son, Matt, shot videos for them. Who knew? I found out at his wake when a woman by the name of Susan appeared a bit lost - as if she was in the wrong place. It turned out that she was the Executive Director of the charity at the time. She was looking for a Matthew but wasn't sure if she had remembered correctly which funeral home she should be at. I told her to approach the casket and let me know. Yep, it was the Matt who shot (pro bono) videos for her Community Adult Day Care Center's social media and web pages. Susan has since retired, and we have a new Exec Director by the name of Elaine Yurjanic. If you're up for it, I'll gladly give you a tour and introduce you to Elaine. Thank you so much for taking Snickers....I'd love to see Matt's cat again - if only for a few moments.*
>
> *Regards,*
>
> *Matt's dad*

I visited Snickers who really didn't pay much attention to me. I couldn't blame her since I didn't know her the way Matt did. Also, it had been a number of years since she started living with Ellen and her family. This was her home. Her safe place. I was basically a stranger.

But the visit gave me a chance to meet Ellen's family. I took a seat at the kitchen table. Ellen served me a cup of tea.

"Do you remember the comments you got when you posted the need for help?"

"Yeah, a lot of mean comments Ellen, from people criticizing me and my son for seeking a home other than ours for Snickers. It wasn't like we were putting the cat in a kill shelter…we just wanted some help for a short while till Matt got back on his feet."

"I couldn't understand that. Why would anyone attack someone trying to be responsible about a pet?" Ellen took a sip from her cup of tea. "Yes, it was mean."

Ellen had met with Matt a number of times. Her home was only about a mile away and I think when Matt was BLUE, he'd drive over to see his Snickers and maybe Ellen. The woman was blessed with a genuinely nice disposition that any troubled soul would want to be around. It was if she had an aura about her and I only remember seeing that once, except that time it was a gentle man with that kind of charm.

My meeting with Ellen, her family and Snickers confirmed to me that good people still made the world go around.

"I liked your son and so did my family. He truly loved Snickers. I'm sorry he didn't make it. I know he struggled. He often wanted to talk, and he didn't hide any of it. That may be what I admired the most about Matt. He didn't harbor any secrets or sugar coat what he considered his sins. I never saw it that way. He was ill, as sick as anyone that might have a physical ailment. His insecurity was all in his mind because he was a good soul." Ellen took another sip of her tea. I did as well. I didn't know what to say.

"I hope you don't mind me saying what I did."

"Not at all. I'm glad he had someone to talk to who cared. I was too consumed with the thought that he had to follow a certain regiment in order to overcome his addiction. I hate to admit it but I think I lost sight of what my son needed…a good listener."

"If it helps, he often spoke of you. He told me that he hoped someday he could grow up and be just like his dad. He really admired your talent as a professional and I'll never forget what he said because it seemed so out of character from someone so young. He said, 'My dad's an ethical dude and I'd be happy if I could live my life that way.'"

"You have no idea Ellen how much that means to me…to hear that. Thank you."

I did take Ellen on a tour of the charity that my son steered me to. She wound up being a volunteer that could relate to older adults with cognitive and physical disabilities. People in that group require a great deal of patience and Ellen had it to give.

I had tears of joy from hearing what Ellen shared even if I didn't shed them in front of her that day. Her insight helped me deal with my melancholy and offered me a bit of hope that brought bliss. Maybe I had been a good father to my son. It was that hope that forced me to live each day with purpose and not give up when the going got rough. God bless that child.

Shayna Rose

She was a girl with rosy cheeks, flaming red auburn hair, a cute figure, blue eyes and a smile that would intrigue any man, be they young or old. She had been the love of his son's life. That the father was sure of. Why did she pick up and take flight in the night to Las Vegas? He could never get the truth from the son when he was alive and figured he'd never discover what had forced her into exile now that his boy was dead.

It was a Facebook post on *simple sister's* page that he discovered when she left her laptop on the kitchen table while she jumped into the shower. He couldn't help but notice that Shayna Rose had returned to Downers Grove and announced the she was working as a barmaid at a place less than a mile from the house. The old man flipped to her profile page and saw photos, lots of them of that cute Shayna Rose hugging a little boy that was the spitting image of his son when he was a toddler.

He had to know. What would be the approach? Did *simple sister* know and even if she did, would she tell?

Maybe it might be best to "friend" Shayna Rose? They certainly knew each other. He had always liked the woman and couldn't understand her sudden departure from his son's life.

What he could remember was Matt in a frenzy dropping by with Shayna and pleading with his father that he give him

$380.00 without explanation. "I need that money dad. I can't tell you why. C'mon, I'll pay you back."

The old man would have given him the money but not without hearing what it was going to be used for. That was definitely 'old school,' but that was the old man who could be and often was suspicious of his son's motives. When the old man didn't fork over the money, the couple left and then Shayna disappeared from sight.

He heard through the grape vine from one of Matt's pals, Brett, that Shayna was in Vegas working as a waitress and going to school. Based on Brett's recollection, Shayna had an uncle that worked in Nevada who let her crash at his place and helped her find a gig. Matt never ever brought up the woman's name again even after he was forced to live with his father or face incarceration for his addiction of opioids that he often accessed illegally.

A Facebook friendship request was sent. Nothing happened for over two weeks. The old man was sure that he might not be accepted and then he was. He grabbed his cell phone and began to shoot some of the cuddly shots of Shayna with that little boy that looked a lot like Matt.

He decided to drop by Bryan's Grille on a Friday night when he knew Shayna would be working. It would require diplomacy. It would require delicacy. How do you ask if your son left a son that his own father knew nothing about? A lot of small talk would need to be made. Maybe it would even be best if he didn't bring the matter up, the first or the second or the third time he visited. It would require some trust and that would require time.

So, he often sat and waited at the bar and made the small talk necessary. It was the fifth visit when he showed the picture, he took from her FB page. He then showed a photo of Matt when he was little and merely waited for a reaction. There was none forthcoming. If Vegas had taught Shayna anything, it was how to maintain a poker face.

The young woman had garnered a college degree. The barmaid gig was merely a way to put a dent in the college loans. She had a beau and marriage was on the horizon and "No, that's not my son, that's my nephew. Why do you ask?"

The man was at a loss for words. He said his good night and exited the bar never to return.

But *simple sister* knew better and she had no intention of breaking her bond. There were some things better left unsaid to protect the living and the dead. It was enough to know that her brother's smile would live on…that was all the bliss she needed.

Forgiven

Hindsight is always to be revered. In hindsight you get to tell yourself how smart or dumb you were at a moment in your life. Hindsight is like looking in a rearview mirror that transports you to what's behind you, what's in the rear of your life, whatever came before will always be gone, never to return. It also comes in handy when you think about someone you lost and at one time loved. Someone that could have been the dawning of a new day for you because the exchange was so unique and memorable.

There was no forgetting Bud. He was a character bigger than life and that came across in person or on that little screen in one's home, known as the Telly, which allowed anyone to think that they knew the guy when in fact, they didn't have a clue.

We worked together as a team. I was his producer for his sports segments on the 6 and the 10 o'clock newscasts that aired in a major Midwest Market which had professional teams in all the major sports: baseball, football, hockey and basketball. People were literally mad when it came to their teams. In a town far from either coast filled with film and TV celebrities, the middle linebacker if he was any good was a big deal – a celeb for sure.

After a number of years together, we parted company due to career moves. Bud decided to give New York, that #1 television

& radio zenith of a market - a try. They threw a lot of money at the man but that wasn't the only reason Bud needed to get away. His heart was crushed by a divorce press that turned all his tears to wine just like grape crush. The man was ready to move far, far, away from the maddening crowd of his personal life.

We each had each other's cell phone numbers, but we never called. A good 15 years passed before we ran into each other unexpectedly in a wine shop of all places. I was happy to see Bud. I asked if I could call him the next day to talk about the possibility of doing some voice over work for a pro bono charitable spot and one for a cash paying client that I was producing. I wasn't even sure if Bud did that kind of work anymore or not. But the reaction was positive; I was welcomed to make the call to discuss the details.

We easily returned to working together on the production of a number of radio and TV commercial voice over spots. On occasion we'd even grab lunch and share a bit of our personnel lives which rekindled what had been a dormant friendship.

And just as easily as we had come together, we moved apart for another five years. There wasn't a reason for alarm, we just drifted which happens when people work together in a freelance world of gigs. Bud was no longer tied with any specific radio or TV outlet. Sometimes his buddies would bring him back to analyze a hot football contest or to provide color for coverage of a playoff run from one of those franchises that attracted such fan frenzy. And as we both got older moving towards the advent of retirement, we still needed to work for our sanity and to ensure that when we did leave the working world, we could do it comfortably. I was aware from mutual colleagues that Bud was busy enough to be okay financially. He had made some big bucks and wisely saved those dollars and on occasion invested some of that green, but very cautiously. There were plenty of speaking engagements for him to do - whether it was some local rotary or as a graduation keynote orator for a high school or college that coughed up 500 or a thousand, respectively, for the booking that secured a charismatic figure like Bud, to be on the dais.

Eventually our paths did cross again. While commissioned to run a vocational college with a broadcast curriculum, I needed a personality that would draw press coverage. Someone from the marketing group suggested that the guy to get for the grand opening should be none other than that wacky, weird, bigger than life kooky sportscaster, Bud. The marketing guys were right. Corporate was pleased and even suggested that I try and find a role for Bud on an ongoing basis.

The students loved having a guy like Bud serve as the Senior Radio Consultant for the school. It was a great deal for Bud. Fifteen hundred a month for two guest speaker appearances on the campus and hosting two one-hour radio shows each week on the Internet radio station owned by the school was a sweet deal for Bud. The man could do the shows with the students from his home studio that had an AEA A440 carbon ribbon microphone with Internet connectivity, which was what he did initially, but that evolved with time as Bud found being around the youthful students a shot in the arm for his psyche. Also, I think Bud needed someplace to go, so he started coming into the campus more and more.

There was a strict policy that the instructors and counselors on staff could not fraternize with the students. If one did that, it was grounds for immediate dismissal. That clause along with a moral's clause was included in the three-year contract afforded Bud by corporate.

I couldn't help but note that Bud's association with the school was a big deal with the fathers of the students recruited by our sales team. It was a private school with a modest tuition that provided for those that qualified for student loan financing. When Bud was on campus, he was always willing to take selfies with the dads or the moms who were part of his fan base and when asked even sign autographs. The man, almost 60, beamed like a little kid does when they're blessed with adulation.

Bud was *somebody* when it came to the students' parents. The parents had at some point in their consumption of radio or TV caught Bud's unpredictable and memorable act. The students worshipped the guy - a leading figure in sports coverage and sports talk radio.

When does the shoe drop? That's all I could think of. When does this wacky character, who I truly liked, do something that I just knew was going to pop up which would make life fuzzy, awkward, or difficult? Maybe when you think like that, you inadvertently bring on a vibe that facilitates *something – something* you really don't want to deal with.

And in a blink of an eye that *something* appeared.

An attractive young woman hired by me to run the receptionist desk and at times perform secretarial work was standing in my doorway. She had her raincoat on armed with an umbrella and I expected the usual refrain before she headed home, "Is there anything you need me to do boss, before I walk out the door?"

But on that *something* of days - those words never surfaced in the space between us. Her eyes told me she was hurting.

"What's up Mindy?"

"May I talk to you privately?" She looked at the door and I nodded for her to close it and take a seat in one of the two armchairs in front of my large mahogany desk.

I waited. I knew she'd eventually open up and after a short silence, she did.

"I'm not sure how to say this." She looked at me with her big brown eyes that were teary eyed.

"Mindy, just say it…we'll figure it out together." She nodded and then let it out as if she was bleeding a tire of all its air.

"I'm tired of Bud pinching my ass and when it's not that then it's touchy-feely-pats-on my-ass, as if I'm just supposed to take that shit. I may be only a receptionist, but I am someone with my own hopes and dreams of working in the biz someday." Since she had been a graduate of one of our sister schools, her hopes and dreams were far from far-fetched. They went with the program.

"Got it. I'll have to do an investigation. Any witnesses that can back you up?"

"Why, do I need them?" I could have dismissed that query as naïve, but I thought better than do that with a woman who was obviously upset. I answered without any hint of sarcasm.

"Because if I know Bud, and I think I do, he's going to deny your claim. And if it comes down to just a *he said/she said* point-counterpoint, you haven't much of a case."

Mindy looked frustrated. Her top lip quivered as she bit her bottom lip. Her eyes watered and the brow of her forehead looked like the hide of a Shar Pei. "Well, there were a few students by the reception desk when he did it this afternoon about 3 p.m. I guess I can talk to them."

"No, absolutely not. Get me the names and I will do the inquisitions. If you were to do them, anyone, including Bud can call them tainted."

A phone rang. "I've got to get this. We'll talk. But know this, I'll have to talk with Bud as well. He's got a side that must be heard." I noticed her look of disdain. "It's only fair." I then picked up the phone and watched Mindy leave.

By the time I talked with Bud, I had a list of the names of students that were by reception on the day Mindy noted on her complaint.

Bud was stalwart that the claim was "nothing but total, unequivocal bullshit my friend. How long have you known me?"

"A long, long, time, but my job requires that I conduct an investigation. Mindy claims she may have witnesses."

"Witnesses, like who?"

I should never have read off the names, but I did, and Bud ran to the bank with it. By the time I got to talk to the four students, not one of them, including the two women would say a word about what they saw or didn't when it came to Bud and Mindy. The first three students seemed as if they had rehearsed how to answer my questions as to whether Bud touched Mindy inappropriately? But the fourth student was a young man of only 17. He had dropped out of high school early after securing a GED, which was all that was required by our vocational college entrance requirements. If he had been prepped, he lost all semblance of the gravity of the alleged infraction. I was astounded that he openly shared a promise Bud had made to him - an internship with one of the major sports radio stations in town.

"And the expectation for that help was expressed to you by Bud how?"

It finally dawned on the young man that he had said way too much.

"Let's keep it simple Adam. Did you see Bud touch Mindy – specifically pat her on her…her ass?"

"No sir. I can't say that I saw that." There was a transparency about the young man. I trusted him. I began to wonder about the validity of Mindy's complaint. In all the years I worked with Bud, no one ever accused him of sexual harassment or inappropriate behavior in the work-place.

I told both the plaintiff and the defendant that I'd conclude my investigation within seven days and then announce a decision that would bring the issue to closure.

The day before I had to reveal my findings, I was on a closed-circuit staff meeting via an Internet stream that had campus directors from all seven of our schools nationwide. I didn't want to even reveal the complaint but thought it best to be transparent. I noted the delicacy of the issue in what we all now had to take seriously in the #metoo era. I expected taunts and criticism from my fellow colleagues for even bringing something like that up on our business conference stream that allowed us to see all seven campus directors a COO and a CEO. To my surprise there was no rebuke in how I had handled the matter. The only question posed was, "How are you going to handle this?"

The Director of IT, also on the video conference, suggested that he might be of service. "Depending on how long ago this incident occurred, I might be able to help you shed some light on what actually happened?"

"Within the last two weeks."

"Oh, well then you're in luck. We have a lipstick camera in that reception area. We have a disc that holds up to 20 days of data. In other words, we record the output of that camera daily. After the call, I'll show you how to get that video coverage and then transfer it to a DVD. It should make for must-see TV." Paul had quite the smile having invoked an old promotional campaign slogan for the NBC TV Network popular back in the day.

Bud was sitting in my office when I came back from lunch on judgment day. I was ready. I'm not sure if deep down I wanted to proceed per my plan of action, but that mattered little. I had to deal with it.

"Hi Bud."

"Hi Chief."

We both looked at each other for a moment when Bud broke the silence.

"So?"

"I spoke to all of Mindy's…witnesses…students…who were up in reception when you also were up there."

"And?"

Bud was too sure of himself. If it hadn't been for Paul's lipstick camera that assurance would never have cracked.

"None of them attested to having seen what Mindy claimed."

Bud had a look that was incredibly rich with a smile that said, "See I told you so."

"So Bud, I guess I'll have to figure out what to do with Mindy."

"Chief, I don't want her to lose her job. We don't need to take it that far. Just a warning and I think we're good."

I nodded.

"Well that's incredibly charitable. I'm pleased to hear that, but could you clear something up for me before you run into a radio studio?"

"Sure Chief, what?"

I turned my laptop so that Bud could see it as I hit play on the DVD control. The screen was filled with the four students, Mindy and Bud. Mindy was at the XEROX machine when Bud with a paper in his hand moved away from a student toward that machine as if he were about to make a copy. The upheld paper blocked the camera's sight but only for a moment; the block didn't cover the action of Bud swiping at Mindy's ass as she collected all of her copies.

I was worried Bud was going to have a stroke.

"Surveillance…is that what it's come to in the workplace?" Bud's assured swagger disappeared, I would have fired the man right then and there, but I left it up to Mindy. I told her that Bud, when he was confident of vindication, expressed a genuine concern that Mindy should not lose her job. I think that somehow touched Mindy.

She took the same tack as Bud. "There's no need for anyone to lose a job, but the man's hands have to be checked at the door when he enters the campus. And I want an apology in the privacy of your office. A simple, 'I'm sorry,' will suffice."

Bud agreed to all of Mindy's terms and conditions. Peace at last.

What I didn't expect was how close the two of them would become as friends and colleagues. Bud invited Mindy to join in on some of the radio shows he was producing. He introduced her to other pros via email introductions and it wasn't long before Mindy handed me her resignation with an ample two-weeks-notice to find a replacement.

Mindy was off to begin her career on the radio. There's little question in my mind that Bud didn't bend over backwards to help the woman find a position on a 50,000-watt radio powerhouse as the weather/traffic reporter. Guilt sometimes has a funny way of bringing out the best in us. Their friendship was like a fine wine. As time went by it got better and better and Bud gave Mindy away at her wedding which I was invited to. Mindy's dad had passed. Sans any uncles or brothers, she picked Bud to walk her down the aisle and that had to be one of the happiest sights in my life, considering how disastrous things could have turned.

Years later, after Bud and I had long departed our roles as educators on that vocational college campus, I bumped into Bud again via the Internet and LINKEDIN. Bud wrote me a private note in which he recalled our moment in the heat of our confrontation. "I never apologized to you and I should have. You did what you had to do when you didn't renew my contract. I get it now even if I was pissed then."

That apology lead to a renewal as grand as the one between Rick Blaine and Captain Renault at the conclusion of that cinema classic, *Casa Blanca* with a line I'll never forget, "Louis (pronounced Louie in French), I think this is the beginning of a beautiful friendship."

Friendship was what we offered each other. The man was there for me when my son disappeared into the shadows.

It was a mere 10 days after having Bud as a storyteller at a charitable fund raiser I was involved with that had a format similar to the MOTH RADIO HOUR where people tell true stories about something poignant or funny or both that I heard the news on the radio. Just for the record, the venue drew a large audience and that was due in part to the fact that Bud still could attract fans who loved hearing his true-life stories.

That's why I hate ending this story with the news that my on-again, off-again, on-again, off-again and on-again friend was killed in an automobile accident. Bud wasn't doing the driving. He was being chauffeured to perform his magic on behalf of a worthy 501c3 that needed support. God bless him because if he won't, I will.

Whenever I remember Bud, I remember two days; the day I met him and the last day I saw him alive…a mere yesterday even if one of those dates sits forty years apart from the other on a calendar. Both of those days brought me great bliss because on those days Bud and I enjoyed what we did for a living and what we did for the living.

GRASP

Grief Recovery After A Substance Passing

The woman and the man sat across from each other waiting for the others. They never arrived.

It was awkward but he couldn't help but think this retired principal had the best of intentions in her quest to set up a grief group. He wouldn't leave. He would stay and talk.

He shared with the woman that he had been to a grief group once before. It was all wrong. "Everyone there had lost a child to cancer or leukemia or a car accident, not one of them lost their kid to an addiction. I felt so out of place."

"Well, you needn't worry with me and I do believe there will be others. We all share in common the fact that our kids, our adult children, left us too early due to their inability to say, 'NO!' They fell into a rabbit hole that neither they, nor we, could help them get out of."

The woman was right. The very next meeting there were an additional ten people besides the father who had lossed his son at only 24 and the group's leader, Terri. They all had in common what it was like to live with an addict. They all shared the depression every parent faced when they had to bury their kid.

Now it was time to crawl out of the shell and if possible, help others who were at a loss. Maybe redemption was possible but only if all that hate was turned around and the man shared his grief and his son's story. He had turned to stone and now it was time to break out of that mold and move on – to live - but only with a purpose that moved on past the dying embers of a nightmare that made joy impossible to know since the boy was gone.

He was asked by a pastor to join another man who also had lost a son and for them to talk openly about the nightmare of addiction at a Sunday service. Lou was the other man. He also lost a son who just couldn't turn the corner.

He was asked by a colleague to say a few words at a memorial for the man's deceased son. "You've been through this… I can't say a thing. You knew my Michael. You knew how good he could be and the promise he had. Please, say a few words."

The man asked to say a few words knew there was no point in asking any more "Why's?" It was a disease that very few understood. He proclaimed to those who would listen, "We need a revolution in how we care for those afflicted by addiction. We need a justice system that doesn't lock them up to merely throw away the key. No, the key to stopping this epidemic is by embracing it. That's what the Portuguese did, and their addiction rates are going down, not up. In Portugal, anyone arrested for drug possession of illegal opioids gets a second chance. They have decriminalized the matter for the user but not the abuser – the drug dealer. The users not only get counseling, but they also get a sponsor that makes a commitment of support for a full two years…to see their charge overcome the addiction and learn a marketable skill, a trade that can help them to put their life back together."

The numbers didn't lie. Portugal had an approach that was radical yet effective. If we could just get rid of the bible thumpers, maybe we could actually wake up in the morning knowing that another 120 didn't die the day before because there was mercy that offered a way out.

That was the insatiable quest he wanted for all the lost souls, even if it was too late for his own flesh and blood who would eventually return some day to his father in a universe where love and bliss were the norm.

Facebook Wars

A post on a Facebook *CLIMATE CHANGE DEBATE PAGE* boldly pronounced that global warming was a scam promoted by a U.N. propaganda unit. Wow! That was the kind of post that would possibly generate a lot of opinions, pro and con. And it did.

I was on the couch with my trusty dog by my side, pleased to have that loyal creature's devotion because frankly my love life was/ has - been a disaster. When I finally found the one-and-only that just wasn't ONLY and then had my heart broken, I felt devastated. And yet I could see my jilter in my arms as we danced through a mythical-white-hot-night-of-passion that was also cool as silk.

Thank goodness there was FB where the disgruntled bash others and frankly move us in ways we didn't even know we should be waiting for. It filled up the time. And so, the comments made by my hand upon my trusty keyboard were not only to vent, provided it was done politely – a self-imposed mandate - but also to conquer the day. Those FB battles can claw at us like that *CLIMAGE CHANGE* post I peered at from outer space…ready to pounce like a ninja assassin.

ADVERSARY: In this group we do not allow the word, "denier," - not nice - and now you must apologize if you want your comment to stand.

ME: Hmmmm… I didn't know I was dealing with "snow-flakes." If it offends you, take it down but do so knowing that the Aussie P.M. actually used "denier" to describe his previous view of global warming only to realize that IT'S REAL. I guess he didn't know the House Rules, LOL!

It continued to gnaw at me. Grasp didn't make it go away. Facebook Wars didn't do me any good even if I often trumped drumpf's uneducated that he professed to love so much.

No, I needed something more. That just wasn't enough no matter how I eviscerated some of those uneducated boobs. I wasn't sure I'd ever find what I was looking for. Happiness sometimes could be that elusive or maybe it was somewhere over a rainbow that one might never find. So I turned to my trusty dog, gave her a pat on her head and accepted her form of a kiss – a lick on my hand. That little gesture gave me all the bliss I needed after executing my FB smackdown.

Happiness Is a Warm Gun

"That's all he told me dad!" The young woman sucked in a deep breath and in rapid fire blurted out, "Yes. he recovered the cell phone and yes, it appears that a deal went down but as the detective said, 'That's not enough to prove that anyone committed a crime....it's all in CODE, and a good defense attorney will make mincemeat out of any possible attempt to indict the dude by the D.A.'"

"Damn, what kind of answer is that? That fuckin' detective's doing nothing. We lost your brother to an asshole who thought it was okay to use a filler known as fentanyl, a poison that should scare anyone beyond belief. I know where Matthew died and once I get that phone back, I'll track that number."

"Good luck with that dad. The detective was worried you might try that. He made it clear that those guys use burner phones. Do you honestly think Matt's dealer is still going to have the phone he used the night Matt connected with him?"

"Yeah, I do. I'll bet he doesn't even know Matt's gone. So yeah. I'm going to find him."

"And then what are you going to do father? It's over. Let it go."

"It's late Pumpkin and I'm not going to get into an argument with you over that low life scum. Besides, I'm upsetting SYD...on the couch next to me by my side." The father looked at his trusty dog before he continued. "Thanks for working with the detective. Oh, before I go, did he say when I can pick up the car from the pound?"

"A couple of days. The police department will issue a letter that will release the car to you without incurring the tow charges or the fines for having it parked in the pound. He'll let me know as soon as he's got it, but for now it's still part of an on-going investigation…he actually said it could be as long as a year before you can go get it." There was an eerie stillness over the cellular waves between them, the kind one hears in the woods just before violence and blood erupt from a buck or a doe if it's not Spring.

"I've got to go dad. I'm sorry but it is what it is. Now please get some rest."

That was the problem; the matter would not rest in peace; the father wouldn't rest in peace. She couldn't help but wonder if something awful was brewing in the wind. But for now, she had to sleep. She had to return to teach her classes the next day upon her return from bereavement leave.

The father had a terrible dream, more like a nightmare. He was walking through a jungle, just like he had in his youth where taking life was expected and even encouraged. Permission had been granted and somehow that made killing acceptable. But this nightmare had narration. It was as if he had caught a National Geographic production on TV filled with the dulcet tones of James Earl Jones.

Father heard the voice of an African man who had a bit of an English accent and it was disconcerting but regally informative. But rather than wake up and escape he just kept moving on in the dream listening even more as if he could really ever expect HOPE to come upon him. The narration flowed as he heard the words babble like a brook:

If you've ever been to Africa and the bush country, then you know that the King of the Jungle, the Lion, only scores 50% of the time when it comes to the need to capture fresh meat.

Lion cubs demand huge quantities of meat. If they don't get it, their chance of survival slips away like a square peg in a round hole. You got to have priorities: My kids, my babies FIRST and damn if I'll play the game differently.

When you really think about it, that percentage – that 50% - is not adequate for survival. That kill-rate was dangerously low and there wasn't any empathy for an animal, scorned by all who lived in the bush.

That's how it was for me, the dealer who serviced Matt that fateful day.

You're asking me to walk away from what I do - to what?

So now I have one more reason to hate you if you come to take away the little, I have. Do I feel bad when I hear one of my clients have crashed and burned? Sure, but in the end they're collateral damage because you allowed me and mine to become collateral damage long, long ago without so much as a thought that maybe you made life impossible for a person of color. Why?

The father knew more than his share of collateral damage. What he had done in his youth one day in that god-awful jungle was beyond redemption. He hadn't meant to squeeze that trigger, but he did, and three little ones were blown to pieces. What he couldn't figure out was how something so heinous could be covered up so easily without consequences. But it was. And within months he was discharged for medical reasons and back home – it was all so hush-hush.

The narration track persisted:

I'm not sure I'd ever seen anyone quite like that Matthew. He also knew music and sound which helped US - make a connection.

I spoke with Matt's old man once. He called me on Matt's phone, so I picked it up. Somehow the old man had figured out what I was to his boy. He threatened to kill me. I pretended that he was out-of-touch with who was who in his son's life and I quickly hung up. But I was certain the old man could or more accurately would kill me if he thought I had endangered his son.

If there was one thing I could count on, it was that when WHITEY said he'd kill you, he wasn't kidding.

And that's when the father woke up. He knew what to do. The dream had revealed it to him.

He'd get that phone back and on that text page, that fatal text, he'd hit the little phone in the corner and become a new customer via Matt, even if Matthew was no longer among the living.

He'd need to talk to someone who could guide him on how to make the order. That wouldn't be all that hard. There were more than enough listed names and numbers; some the father even recognized as friends who had been sucked into that same rabbit hole with his son.

He plotted. He cajoled. And he got what he needed.

He made the call and convincingly made an order as he journeyed down that motorway to the damned, known otherwise as the Eisenhower Expressway which took him to Chicago's dark west side. He wasn't traveling alone. He had his GLOCK-19 that was snub nosed and concealable.

By the time the dealer realized he had fallen into a trap, it was too late. The bullet had left the chamber and penetrated a heart and in a ghetto of shadow, that explosion startled no one.

The next day the detective assigned to Matt's case came to the father's door. He knocked three times and was genuinely surprised when the father let him in.

The detective wasted no time.

"I know what you did. You need not say a word and for fuck's sake, don't! You did us all a favor, but I suppose I'm politically incorrect for saying that, but I'm exhausted from all this shit…I just don't give a damn anymore."

The father merely nodded. He wanted the detective to know that he acknowledged the man's ability to ferret out the truth regarding the victim now turned ghost. Had he been directly asked to respond to a question of guilt, he was more than willing to admit his sin. It would have been the ethical thing to do. But his confession wasn't welcome even though he had strayed.

The sweet smell of success might be only temporary, and it might cause his fall from grace in the eternal hereafter but like the detective, he also was exhausted.

Did it really matter? The father was convinced that what he had done in the jungle long, long ago had sealed his fate anyway with the Almighty. The SHAME of that day was the one and only secret he kept from his Pumpkin. Even when it had become cool to acknowledge appreciation, he hid from it. That SHAME was a sin he didn't want his beloved daughter to somehow unravel unlike his revenge for his failure to protect one of his own. Who knew? She might actually have tolerated that sin of retribution. The father's world had been tossed upside down.

In his head, he saw a woman by the side of a road who paralyzed the father with fear. It was his mother who had passed many moons ago who was crying tears weighted with the knowledge that her pride and joy was lost…suffering from a shade of pale he would never recover from.

Father found bliss the only way he knew how – in this perverted case, happiness came via a warm gun even if it meant he was on the road to hell. The shadows dancing on the walls when he saw himself making his trip down the River Styx would not be offset by a dog with a shiny tail. No, he had crossed a line and now he had to live with it, but if that meant keeping *simple sister* safe than so be it, he'd live with what he had done and what he had failed to do.

But it sure beat the feelings he had when Mr. Blue came around, because that was the worst. Perhaps his sin was the only thing that gave him any kind of bliss, and bliss like beauty was in the mind of the beholder, but sadly the question nagged him with each day that passed before he made that trip to the other side.

Why did the SON have to die so young? He waited for an answer from the FATHER or the HOLY GHOST but all he was left rattling within his head was a reverberating - Why?

Acknowledgements

I want to thank those who helped me in the creation and development of *Stories Unified in Bliss,* a set of stories that can be read individually but collectively are connected. Specifically, I'd like to express my gratitude to Renee Rosen, James Riordan, Mary Ann Presman, Renee Gonzalez, Peanut and Sydney.

About the Author

WillIam (Bill) Natale, is an Emmy-Award winning producer/director and executive member of the Directors Guild of America Midwest Council. He is the author of *"1968 – A Story As Relevant Today As It Was Then,"* and a children's book, entitled *"Woolly Wurm,"* that was written specifically to help raise funds for The Infant Welfare Society of Chicago. Natale's new book, *"The Resurrection of Boraichee,"* debuted August 1, 2020, and is available in bookstores as well as AMAZON & KINDLE.

Natale has served as the Executive Director of the Illinois Center for Broadcasting/IL Media School, Chicago Campus;

Executive Producer of Internet Streaming Corporation and Executive Producer of WATCH312.COM.

Natale served for over 4 years as president of the board of directors for PanAmerica Performance Works Theater Company (formerly Latino Chicago Theater Company). He has served as a member of the board of directors for the Chicago chapter of the National Association of Television Arts & Sciences and as Chairman of the Broadcast Promotion & Marketing Executives Association. Natale serves as an advisor to the board of directors for the 501-c *BIBO AWARDS FOUNDATION*, (Beauty In & Beauty Out) that honors outstanding women for their community service in the Chicago, Las Vegas and Los Angeles metropolitan areas. He also serves on the board of directors for the 501-c *SHINE ON CHICAGO* organization that teaches inner-city children how to shoot, produce and edit video that can then be shared via social media and is currently president of the Board of Directors for the 501c, The Community Adult Day Care Center (CADC) in Downers Groves.

Natale became aware of CADC via videos shot pro bono by his son Matthew. Some time later CADC proved to be a GODSEND for his sister, a care giver for his brother-in-law who suffered from both cognitive and physical disabilities and was served by the wonderful staff at CADC prior to his passing in 2020.

Carissa and his grandson Grey live with him in Downers Grove where he has resided for the last 28 years. He has been blessed to have two other daughters, Gina and Renee and a son, Matthew - who passed away in 2017.